"We can't stay here. ~~I think~~ our being here has scared whoever is after you past the point of caution. We're sitting ducks."

"And how are we supposed to leave? And, even if we do leave, where would we go? The power is still down and the creek's still flooded," Jess countered.

She had a point. The situation wasn't ideal. "We're just going to have to rough it," he announced.

Her brows lowered. Her teeth gnawed at her full lower lip. "Seth."

"Yeah?"

"We're about five miles out from where Rebecca's parents live."

"Do you trust her family?"

"Yeah. I'm sure her family would help us if we could just get to their house."

He considered it. "Where do they live?"

She told him. "Most of the houses on their street are owned by the Amish. And the lumber mill Levi works at is close by. We could probably get over there and use the business phone to call the police."

"Better there than here. If we can sneak into the woods without being seen, we have a chance."

He waited for her slow nod.

"Let's do it."

Dana R. Lynn grew up in Illinois. She met her husband at a wedding and told her parents she had met her future husband. Nineteen months later, they were married. Today they live in rural Pennsylvania with their three children, two dogs, one cat, one rabbit, one horse and six chickens. In addition to writing, she works as an educational interpreter for the deaf and is active in several ministries in her church.

Books by Dana R. Lynn

Love Inspired Suspense

Amish Country Justice

Plain Target

Presumed Guilty
Interrupted Lullaby

Visit the Author Profile page at Harlequin.com.

PLAIN TARGET

DANA R. LYNN

HARLEQUIN® LOVE INSPIRED® SUSPENSE

If you purchased this book without a cover you should be aware that this book is stolen property. It was reported as "unsold and destroyed" to the publisher, and neither the author nor the publisher has received any payment for this "stripped book."

Recycling programs for this product may not exist in your area.

LOVE INSPIRED BOOKS

ISBN-13: 978-0-373-45702-1

Plain Target

Copyright © 2017 by Dana Roae

All rights reserved. Except for use in any review, the reproduction or utilization of this work in whole or in part in any form by any electronic, mechanical or other means, now known or hereinafter invented, including xerography, photocopying and recording, or in any information storage or retrieval system, is forbidden without the written permission of the editorial office, Love Inspired Books, 195 Broadway, New York, NY 10007 U.S.A.

This is a work of fiction. Names, characters, places and incidents are either the product of the author's imagination or are used fictitiously, and any resemblance to actual persons, living or dead, business establishments, events or locales is entirely coincidental.

This edition published by arrangement with Love Inspired Books.

® and TM are trademarks of Love Inspired Books, used under license. Trademarks indicated with ® are registered in the United States Patent and Trademark Office, the Canadian Intellectual Property Office and in other countries.

www.Harlequin.com

Printed in U.S.A.

My God will fully supply whatever you need,
in accord with His glorious riches in Christ Jesus.
–Philippians 4:19

This book is dedicated to the memory of my Aunt Norma, who first introduced me to the genre of romance, sparking a lifelong fascination with Happy Ever Afters.

Acknowledgments:

Although writing is a solitary career, I couldn't do it without the love and support of so many people. First, to my wonderful husband, Brad, and our kids. You alternately kept me sane and drove me crazy during this process, and I wouldn't have it any other way!

To my editor, Elizabeth Mazer, who took the time to brainstorm with me to make this story come to life. You are awesome, and I am so grateful to be able to work with you.

A special bittersweet thanks to my late agent, Mary Sue Seymour, who passed away before this book was completed. She loved this project and cheered me on from the beginning. A woman of great faith, energy and kindness. I was truly blessed to have been able to work with her.

My heartfelt gratitude to my Lord and Savior. I pray that my words will always point to Your love and mercy.

ONE

"Fire!"

Jess McGrath tore the fire extinguisher off the wall before running back to the blaze in her brother's office. For the first time in five weeks she entered the room where she had found Cody dead from his own hand. Behind her, her hearing aids caught the eruption of sound as her visitors, Rebecca and Levi Miller, scurried to help the two daytime workers release the horses into the pasture. Gratitude surged briefly. Rebecca was her oldest friend. No one else had stuck by her when the scandal started, leading to Cody's disgrace and the near ruin of their training stables. Her Amish-raised friend didn't even consider abandoning Jess. It was fortunate that Rebecca had persuaded her indulgent older brother to give her a ride in to visit Jess today on his buggy. With staff down to the bare-bones minimum, Jess needed all the help she could get.

Pulling the pin, Jess aimed the extinguisher at the flames consuming the exterior wall. Would it be enough?

Please Lord, let everyone and the horses be safe.
The pictures on the wall connected to the stalls vibrated

as the horses were led out. They would go directly to the pasture.

The flames died out and the extinguisher sputtered as it emptied. Jess stared at the destruction before her. Cody's desk had taken the brunt of it, along with the wall. How had it started? The electrical systems had all been updated within the past three years. And no one had been in the office for weeks.

Not since the police had taken all Cody's files when he came under suspicion for various charges of fraudulent practices. A third of the clientele to the stables and training facilities she owned with her brother had taken their business, and their horses, elsewhere. River Road Stables was facing bankruptcy if she didn't find a way to improve business.

Her eyes landed on the still smoldering heap that had been a garbage can. It was unrecognizable. Only the fact that Jess knew what it should be helped her identify it. Her stomach turned. Trembling began from her toes up. Had the fire started there?

The floor vibrated, almost a heaving feeling. Jess spun around in time to see the large bookcase rock forward. The frame was anchored to the wall, but she could see the screws being ripped out. Even as she jumped out of its way, she knew she hadn't jumped far enough. The heavy shelf toppled, knocking into her as it fell. She crashed to the ground. A sharp pain exploded in her head.

Jess struggled to open her eyes. The left side of her face ached. Her ears rang. With a groan, she lifted her head, only to drop it as nausea rolled over her.

A warm hand patted her shoulder. She risked opening her eyes again. A paramedic loomed over her, a concerned frown digging furrows in his forehead. He looked vaguely familiar. Her head ached too much to wonder where she had seen him before.

"Jessica? Jess, can you hear me?"

She blinked, incredulous. Who was this man? She had to have met him somewhere. Not only did he know her name, but he had also signed as he spoke. Of course, she was wearing her hearing aids, so it wasn't fully necessary. It was appreciated all the same.

She moved her head. Oww.

"My head hurts," she moaned.

He nodded, watching her carefully. "I think you may have a concussion. We'll know better once a doctor examines you. I did check your vitals. They look good." He continued to sign while he spoke.

"How did you know I'm deaf?"

His eyes widened, a surprised expression crossing his face. Followed immediately by a guilty one. His gaze shifted nervously before returning to rest on her face again.

"You don't recognize me?" He seemed wary of her answer.

She shook her head slowly, wincing as her aching head protested. "No, but you look really familiar."

He sighed. "High school."

It couldn't be.

Narrowing her eyes, she looked closer. It was. How had she not recognized him? But he had changed so much from the gangly sixteen-year-old boy she had known so briefly eleven years ago. His black curly hair was shorter, and his scrawny body had shot up in height and was well muscled. The nerdy glasses were gone. But the eyes…she did remember them. Deep brown eyes that she had crushed on for several months during her freshman year before realizing that the sweet boy she thought she knew didn't exist. He had been a bad boy who was only interested in flaunting the rules and irritating his high-society parents.

"Seth Travis." The words felt bitter on her tongue.

He nodded, then focused his attention off himself. "Do I need to sign, or can you hear me well enough if I just talk? I can help you faster if I don't sign."

"Yeah, as long as I have my hearing aids on and it's quiet and I can see your face, I'm good."

"I remember that."

Of course he did. Seth had always been brilliant. On track to be the salutatorian. Not to mention his memory. She had been amazed at his ability to recall even the smallest of details. She didn't remember him signing in high school, though. When had he learned? And why bother?

"I'm surprised you didn't recognize me. What with my dad being the senator and all."

She shrugged. "It's been a long time since I saw you and you've changed a lot. And I don't pay attention to politics. Never have."

"So you never saw my old man on television?" His mouth curled in a slight sneer. Problems with his dad, apparently. It was none of her business, but she couldn't say she approved of his attitude. She would never have disrespected her parents that way.

"I don't own a TV." She didn't add that she had better things to do with her time than to watch the drama of the spoiled rich kid she remembered play out before her.

Rebecca entered the stables, and Jess settled her attention on her dearest friend. Rebecca's brother, Levi, followed her at a slower pace. It still looked odd to see Rebecca dressed *Englisch* when she stood next to her Amish brother. But it warmed her heart, too, knowing that Rebecca's family supported her choices. Jess knew that Rebecca's social circle was very small, due in part to her deafness. It could have been smaller. If she had left her community after she'd been baptized, she would have been shunned, even by her family. The fact that she had decided to leave her Amish community instead of being baptized had enabled her to keep her close ties to her family.

"Is everyone okay? The horses?" Jess signed to Rebecca, who was born profoundly deaf. Unlike Jess, Rebecca depended totally on American Sign Language, or ASL. People were always surprised to find out how little she could lip read. English was a difficult language to lip read well, with so many sounds looking the same on the lips. Add the fact that Rebecca's family spoke Pennsylvania Dutch at home into the mix, it was no wonder she hadn't bothered with it.

"Yes. We helped your two employees move them to the back pasture. How are you? I was scared when I found you unconscious." Rebecca's hands flew.

Jess looked at Seth. Did he need her to interpret? Her mouth fell open when he answered Rebecca in almost fluent ASL. That was a whole different skill set than putting signs to English grammar. She was impressed in spite of herself.

"My partner and I need to take her to the hospital," he signed, indicating someone behind her.

Jess hadn't even noticed the other paramedic. The

woman walked their way, pushing a stretcher. She gave Jess a professional smile.

Jess turned her attention back to Rebecca and Levi. "Did anyone call the fire department?"

They both shook their heads. "We didn't think it was necessary," Levi answered her. "The fire was out. It was *gut, jah*?"

No surprise there. Calling for outside help would not enter Levi's mind unless it was absolutely crucial.

She hesitated. Part of her was relieved not to have to handle the firefighters or police. She had dealt with so much scandal recently, she didn't have the heart to face more. But the other part of her wondered if the fire was an accident. It just seemed odd that it started in Cody's office for no apparent reason.

A stretcher halted on her left side. The female paramedic had reached their small group.

"I called the fire department a few minutes ago." The blond woman leaned over to check something on the stretcher. "It's not uncommon for a fire to restart hours after it's put out. It's pretty standard procedure to have the local fire department check it out."

So there was no longer any choice. Jess sighed. She just wanted this day to be over. Quickly, she murmured a prayer for strength. Seth gave her a startled glance, but didn't comment. Instead, he and his partner loaded her into the ambulance and whisked her off to the hospital.

Two hours later, she was receiving her release papers and, except for a lingering headache, a clean bill of health. What was unexpected was that Seth reappeared as she was getting ready to leave with Rebecca. And with him was a police officer. A very grim-faced officer.

"Jess, this is Sergeant Jackson from the LaMar Pond Police Department. He needs to speak with you for a minute." He signed the introductions, then started to back away.

Without thought, her hand shot out and caught at his. "Stay. Please."

He raised his eyebrows, but nodded. She closed her eyes, feeling some of the tension in her chest disintegrate. As little as she trusted Seth, he was someone she knew. Being alone with a police officer was a frightening prospect for her. All she could think of were the accusations of fraud and theft, not to mention the thorough searches she'd endured, that had happened both before and after Cody's death. No matter how much she and Cody had protested that he hadn't stolen money from his foundation or rigged horse races, no one believed them. And even knowing the police were just doing their job didn't shake her feeling that they looked at her with suspicion.

Plus, she reasoned, Seth signed, which could help. As well as she read lips, she sometimes needed to see the words to be sure she understood them. And interpreters were hard to find. She could be here hours if she waited for one.

Sergeant Jackson cleared his throat. "Miss McGrath, the fire department investigated the fire at the stables. It's their inspector's opinion that the fire might have been deliberately set."

A shiver worked its way up her spine. Her day had just gotten much worse.

Gravel crunched under the tires of Seth's Ford pickup truck as he turned into the driveway of River Road Stables the next morning. Water splashed up on his tires. The heavy scent of wet hay slipped through the inch-wide crack in his window. It had stormed the night before, and puddles were everywhere. His front tire hit a particularly deep puddle, and he was jarred by the motion as his truck bounced. Man, they really needed to fix the potholes on this driveway.

A yawn crept up on him. He had barely been able to sleep last night. The image of Jess's distraught face haunted him. A queasy sensation settled in his stomach as he realized that the only reason she wasn't being investigated for possibly causing the fire was because of her injury. Yet. He had seen the look in Gavin Jackson's eyes. And he had been around cops enough to know that often arson was committed for insurance fraud.

He expected to continue up the lane to find Jessica in her one-story ranch house where she should be resting, as per doctor's orders. His plan shifted when he spotted her brown ponytail swaying as she walked into the barn. Pressing his lips together, he parked his truck in front of the barn. Frustration and worry mingled. As hard as it was to believe, she didn't have a concussion from her accident yesterday. Still, he was sure she probably was feeling some aches and pains. Enough to convince most people to take it easy and rest. A sigh escaped. Not that he was surprised that she refused to slow down. She always had pushed herself harder than others around her. In his mind, he had always wondered if she felt that being deaf, she had to overachieve in order to prove herself.

To be fair, she had probably been right. He could remember the one class they had together—biology. The teacher had tried to convince her to drop the class, telling her in front of her peers that he didn't have time to waste trying to keep her caught up.

But she had been stubborn. And the guidance counselor had asked Seth to tutor her, to ensure her success. He'd agreed, reluctantly, knowing it would look good to the teachers and guidance counselors who would eventually write him college recommendation letters. And soon found that they had all underestimated her. Had started to admire her, to like her—and that was where the trouble had begun.

He winced. Those were memories he didn't want to relive.

Parking the truck, he grabbed the wallet he had found on his floorboard that morning. If she had noticed it missing, she might be panicking about now. It gave him the excuse he needed to pay her a visit, although he refused to think about why he was so anxious to see her again. He was a paramedic—it was his job to worry about people, particularly people who had just been injured. He had been skeptical when she had agreed to follow the doctor's directives. Something told him that she wouldn't be able to sit still. He had seen the stubborn look in her eyes.

Obviously he had been right.

Didn't she know she needed to rest? He admitted to himself that he was concerned. Working alone in the barn was not safe for her. And she had said the day before that no one would be coming in until after lunch. It hadn't struck him until he had dropped her off that someone—meaning her—would have to come out to take care of the horses in the morning. All alone like that, she would be an easy target if the person who'd attacked her stables came back. He shook off the thought.

For all he knew, the fire was a random act by a group of kids. Yeah, right.

The stable door was standing open. He headed that way, pausing just inside it. Jessica stood outside the office door, her arms closed tight against her belly, her eyes squeezed shut. He started, ready to rush in and… what? Comfort her? He wasn't sure, but he knew he didn't like seeing her so vulnerable. Never had, even though their association had been so brief. Which made what had happened even more contemptible. When he had betrayed her trust, he had left her open to the cruelty of others. It didn't matter that he hadn't been a part of the actions they had taken against her. He knew what a soft heart she had. And that she had a crush on him. But instead of protecting her, he'd stepped back and allowed her to be hurt in a disaster which ended with her being pulled from the school.

He drew himself away from his painful memories. Then he noticed her lips were moving. She was praying. Okay, now he felt really uncomfortable. He wasn't big on prayer. Not that he minded other people praying. He just hadn't had much experience with it personally. And to be honest, he rather doubted it did any good.

A few seconds later she opened her eyes. They widened as she saw him poised in the doorway.

"Seth! What are you doing here?" Her voice was low and pleasant. Although her inflections were slightly irregular, most people probably wouldn't even pick up on that.

"You left this in my truck." He waved the bright pink wallet at her.

Jess's hazel eyes widened. "Oh, no! I hadn't even noticed it was missing."

"No worries. It was safe. And I'm even a little glad 'cuz it gave me an excuse to check up on you. Make sure you were taking it easy." He gave her a pointed look.

She bit her lip. Dropping her gaze to the floor, she scuffed the toe of her boot in the dirt. When she flicked her glance back up to his face, he was momentarily distracted by her wide hazel eyes. He hadn't let himself feel attracted to a woman for a long time. His behavior in high school, and his poor judgment six years ago with his former fiancée, had taught him that he was not husband material. As bitter as it made him feel, he had been forced to acknowledge that he was too much like his father. Selfish and prone to hurt those close to him. Shaking himself out of it, he asked, "What's wrong?"

He held his breath while he waited to see if she would answer. He wouldn't blame her if she brushed him off. She had no reason to trust him. Past events would tell her not to. But he really hoped she would.

Finally, she sucked in a deep breath. Let it out slowly.

"You know that the police are toying with the idea that I started the fire?" She waited for him to nod before she continued. "What I couldn't tell the officer last night was the fire wasn't the first accident."

"What?" He hadn't meant to shout, but her words terrified him. He wanted to sweep her into his truck and drive her to a safe place. The feeling surprised him. And made him uncomfortable.

Jess squirmed. Then she lifted her chin and seemed to collect herself. "I didn't realize at first that they were anything more than accidents. I put it down to carelessness. Until last week. A new ladder broke when I took it out to paint. That's when I started to wonder if someone was behind the accidents. Then this happened."

"How long has this been going on?" He kept his voice calm with an effort.

"About three weeks."

"You should have mentioned it to Sergeant Jackson last night," Seth admonished her.

Hazel eyes blazed up at him. "And you think he would believe me? Just when my barn suffers extensive fire damage and I'm a person of interest?"

She had a point. It would have looked like she was lying to cover her tracks.

"I think it started because I was asking too many questions."

He wasn't going to like this. "Asking questions about what?"

Those soft lips started to tremble. She squished them together. "I know that people think my brother was guilty of something, what with him dying the way he did and all. But I can't believe that of him. He was the most gentle, sincere person I have ever known. I have been trying to find evidence to take to the police to clear his name."

He knew something dicey had happened, although he was foggy on all the details.

"What is it that they think he'd done, exactly?"

For a long moment, she stood, jaw clenched. Clearly it wasn't a topic she enjoyed discussing, and he felt a twinge of guilt for even bringing it up. But he needed to know what they were dealing with if he was going to help her.

"My brother had started a rescue foundation for abused racehorses. Several months ago, one of his volunteers noticed that money was being stolen. The police suspected Cody. The fact that he spent so much time at the race track was suspicious. I guess there was suspicion that he was using funds to support a gambling habit. They questioned him, and there was an investigation. It was never closed. Cody was never even officially charged—they didn't have enough evidence against him. But when he took his own life, everyone seemed to take that as an admission of guilt. People who had contributed to the foundation felt hurt, betrayed. I can understand that," she admitted, "but that doesn't mean I'm all right with people continuing to say such horrible things about him when no one has been able to provide a scrap of evidence proving that he did anything wrong."

"So you spoke up in his defense," Seth concluded, "both when he was first questioned, and then later after his death. And that's turned people against you?"

She nodded.

"Including the police?" he asked.

"Especially the police. Not only was I unable to convince them he was innocent, they made it clear that I was also on their radar, since I worked for the foundation in a minor role. They wouldn't listen to me."

Frustrated, he shoved a hand through his hair. "You have to let the police know about the other accidents, Jess. This is no joke."

She started to shake head. "Don't you understand? There is no way they will believe me! And the stables are already losing clients. If these things keep happening, then I will have to sell the horses and the stable." Tears shimmered in her eyes. "Seth, owning a training stable has been my dream for as long as I can remember. I have already lost my brother. I can't lose this, too."

A constriction formed in his throat. It was necessary

to swallow several times to ease the tightness. A sudden thought popped into his head.

"Wait a minute! Jess, my brother-in-law is a lieutenant in the LaMar Pond Police Department. You can talk to him." Why hadn't he thought of that earlier? Dan was pretty easygoing. And he was head-over-heels ridiculously in love with Seth's half sister Maggie, which meant he'd do just about anything Seth asked—including hearing Jess out, and giving her the benefit of the doubt.

"I didn't know you had siblings." There was that suspicious look on her face again. He was going to have to work hard to earn her trust.

"It's a long story. But Maggie is my half sister. I met her almost a year ago for the first time, but we've gotten close. And her husband, Dan, is a good guy."

A humorless laugh left her mouth. "I can't believe I'm considering listening to you. Seth, we knew each other in high school, but that was eleven years ago. And you betrayed my trust back then. Why should I give it to you now?"

Why, indeed.

TWO

Seth's teeth snapped together with a loud click. He knew his jaw would ache later. Turning away from Jess, he began to pace as he battled to keep the anger and fear simmering beneath the surface from exploding out of him. The temper he had learned to keep under wraps for so long threatened to overwhelm him. It wouldn't do anyone any good to lose it now.

When he had himself under control, he faced Jess again. She eyed him warily.

"Are you okay?" she asked.

Unbelievable. He rolled his eyes.

"Am *I* okay? I'm not the one whose stable was set on fire and I haven't been the victim of any strange accidents. I'm amazed you're not a basket case right now."

Jess shrugged. Her attempt at nonchalance didn't fool him. She was scared. He had to admire her determination to tough it out on her own.

But enough was enough.

"Jess." He took a step closer. Close enough to smell her perfume. Her eyes widened. He needed to make sure he was completely understood. "Come with me to my sister's house. My brother-in-law is off today so we should be able to talk with him in private."

He braced himself to argue with her. Turned out, he didn't need to. She met his eyes, and slowly nodded her head. Reluctant surrender was written all over her face.

"Will you stay? Just in case I need an interpreter?"

Why did he think she actually wanted him there for moral support? She didn't say it, but the plea was in her shadow-filled eyes.

"I won't leave your side," he promised.

Some of the tension drained from her shoulders, and the corners of her lips tilted in a slight smile. The urge to comfort her with a hug crept up, but he resisted. The last thing she would want would be to be touched by him. He was well aware of the fact that he had a long way to go to make up for the jerk he'd been eleven years ago.

Leading her out to his truck, he held the door while she pulled herself up into the cab. Good thing he hadn't parked next to a puddle. As he shut the door behind her and jogged around to his side, he ignored the anticipation dancing through him at the thought of spending more time in her presence. It wasn't as if they were going on a picnic. It started to rain again once they were underway. The overcast sky and the loud patter of raindrops on the roofs made the space inside the cab seem close. The fragrance of her light perfume added to the impression. Perfume? Since when did he pay attention to perfume unless it was too strong? Weird. Just weird.

He glanced into the rearview window, frowning at a car riding right on his tail. "Back up, buddy," he muttered. Seth slowed the car, then made a right turn. The dark green sedan continued to keep pace with him. The tinted glass made it difficult to see who was driving the vehicle. Someone was in a hurry.

"What?"

He shot a reassuring grin at Jess. "Sorry. Talking to myself. We have a tailgater."

Jess looked back over her shoulder, and froze. Seth stopped grinning as he saw the look of fear on her face. Her hands were fisted on her lap, the knuckles white.

"Jess? Jessica! What's wrong?"

"I have seen that car almost everywhere I have gone in the past couple of weeks. I can never tell who's driving it."

The thought of someone shadowing her, stalking her, set his teeth on edge. "Are you sure it's the same car?" He used one hand to sign the question so there would be no mistake.

Jess shook her head. "Sure? No, I have never gotten close enough to see a license plate. And there are hundreds of cars that look like that one. Except for the dark windows."

Without considering his actions, Seth spun the wheel and started to pull off onto the berm. The green car slowed down. Then it suddenly shot forward. Its tires hit a large puddle, and water splashed Seth's windshield. His left hand shot out to activate the wipers, hoping to clear his view in time to get a glimpse of the license plate, but it was too late. The car whipped around the corner. And another car was coming far too fast for Seth to get back on the road and follow him.

Frustrated, he waited for the other car to pass and then resumed driving toward Maggie and Dan's house. His mind was full of questions. And doubts. Was it possible Jess was being stalked, or was she letting her anxiety rule her thoughts? After all, even she had admitted the car wasn't an uncommon model. Except for the windows. He rejected the idea that she was imagining things almost as soon as it entered his mind. She had always been very down to earth, never one to exaggerate or jump to conclusions. "Okay, we need to remember to tell Dan about the car."

Out of the corner of his eye, he saw her nodding, but her expression remained troubled. It was time to see if they could make some sense of the current situation, while they were alone. And the quiet of the truck meant she would be able to hear him. And if she couldn't, it was light enough that she could see him sign, or read his lips if necessary.

"Why don't we try and get our ducks in a row before talking to Dan. He's going to want to know about the people you work with at the barn. Because chances are good that one of them might be the person responsible for the fire."

A shake of her head denied any such possibility, but shadows crept into her expression. As much as she might want to believe none of her coworkers would hurt her, the doubt had taken root in her mind.

"So who worked for you yesterday?" Man, he hated doing this to her. But it was necessary for her protection, he argued with himself.

For a moment, he wasn't sure if she would answer. Finally she sighed. "Kim and Eric. They're both fairly young. Kim just started working for us about seven months ago, but Eric has been coming for years, first as a student, and later as a worker and part-time trainer. I would trust him without hesitation."

"And Kim?"

He knew the answer the moment she bit her lower lip. As painful as it was, Kim was a possible suspect.

"Okay, how about Rebecca—"

The words weren't even out of his mouth before she interrupted him.

"Don't even go there. I would trust her and Levi with my life. We went to the same deaf and hard-of-hearing program for years. In fact, we rode the same bus. She was two years behind me, but we stayed friends even after I returned to my home district for high school."

He nodded. "Okay. And she was Amish?"

"Yeah. Until she was seventeen. She made the choice to leave instead of being baptized, which means she can still visit her family."

"But still, there would have been years when you didn't see her because you left..." His voice petered out as he realized what he was saying. The last thing he wanted to do was bring up why she had left high school, and his role in all of it, but it was too late now. If he could, he would have swallowed those words back. But he couldn't. Maybe she would let it go. He glanced at her. Her lips tightened, her shoulders grew stiff. Nope.

"Yeah, I left to go back to my district's school so I could be closer to home and take advantage of the clubs and sports programs. Things most high school students take for granted. I just didn't expect that to include you telling your bully friends that the weird deaf girl you tutored had an annoying crush on you. And I definitely didn't expect them to decide to teach me a lesson to show me how unworthy I was."

"I never meant—"

"They ganged up on me, drew the word *IDIOT* on my forehead with a permanent marker and shoved me into a dark janitor's closet. It was small, no lights and no windows, and I missed my bus. I was stuck in that small, smelly place for five hours until my parents and the principal found me. I was terrified to go back there. And Rebecca had left the deaf program. Amish students only go to school through eighth grade. I convinced my parents to send me to the Western PA School for the Deaf so I wouldn't have to face any of my attackers again."

So that's where she had gone.

He could hear her ragged breathing. Remorse choked him. What a moron he had been.

"I would do anything to take that back. I only said something to get my girlfriend, Trish, off my back. She was jealous of the time we spent together."

She grimaced. "She was cruel. All your friends were. Except that dark haired girl you sat with in bio."

Melanie. His best friend. He'd messed that up, too.

He sighed, wishing he could go back in time and shake some sense into the stupid, arrogant kid he used to be. "I couldn't believe Trish would do something like that. We had a huge fight over it and finally broke up. I wanted to track you down and apologize…but no one knew where you'd gone."

"How hard did you look?" she asked, her voice cold and accusatory.

"Not very," he admitted. "I figured you wanted to leave me and everything I'd done in the past. It didn't seem right to force you to have to sit through my sad excuses if you'd moved on with your life."

"And yet here you are."

"To help," he insisted. "I know it doesn't change the past, but you're in trouble now and you shouldn't be forced to deal with it alone. I'd like to help you, the way I should have back then."

Silence settled between them, tense and awkward. After a few minutes, he felt her hand touch his arm. Brow rising in surprise, he turned to face her.

"Can I ask you a question?" Jess's voice was hesitant. It was an olive branch, and he knew it and gladly seized it.

"Yeah, sure." His voice was thick. He cleared his throat. He spared her a glance to be sure she heard him. Her face was turned toward him, eyes intent.

"I don't remember ever seeing you sign before. But yesterday you were signing like you'd been doing it for years. How did you learn? Why?"

He shrugged. "I had a roommate in college who was deaf. Ernie. He taught me some sign. And I went home with him several times. His whole family was deaf, so it was sink or swim. After I decided that I had zero interest in following my dad into law and politics, I took other classes to find what interested me. Including ASL."

"Ernie Mitchell?"

His eyebrows rose. "You know him?"

"He attends Deaf church with me."

The mention of church was unsettling. He and Ernie had stayed in touch since college but they didn't talk religion much. Seth blew out a relieved breath as his sister's house came in view. Soon, he would be able to tell Dan everything. Then the police could take control of the situation. Jess would be safe and would no longer need him. That last thought made him frown. The idea of walking away from her now when she was in danger didn't sit well with him at all. But sticking around held the risk of his becoming attached to her. He realized that he liked and admired her. The last thing he wanted was to see her hurt again. And he would hurt her. How could he not? He was his father's son, after all.

Pulling into his sister's driveway, he frowned, feeling uneasy. Dan's truck was there, but the minivan was nowhere in sight. And the blinds were closed. Maggie always opened the blinds. Getting out of his truck, he walked over to the garage and peered in. The motorcycle was there, but no van.

Whipping out his cell, he sent his sister a text. Hey sis. Where r u?

A minute later he received an answer. And groaned. Pittsburg. Visiting Ty. Back 2morrow. Everything OK?

Ty was Dan's foster brother. What now? He would just have to keep an eye on Jess until Dan returned. He sent back a text to tell his sister he needed to see Dan as soon as they returned. Then he climbed back in his truck. Jess was watching him, those gorgeous hazel eyes wide and curious. How would she react to the news that she'd have to wait to talk with Dan? Would she give up on speaking to the police altogether?

"Okay. Change of plans. Maggie and Dan are in Pittsburg for the day."

A soft sigh came from the woman beside him. Relief or resignation? Hmm. Not sure he knew.

"Do you want to go back to your place?" he offered. Man, he hated the thought of bringing her back to that ranch house alone. The stables were far too secluded. Her face paled.

Taking a deep breath, Jess squared her shoulders and lifted her jaw. Probably trying to look brave. To his sympathetic eye, she looked vulnerable. And scared. As she glanced up, her posture shifted. Eyes narrowing, she looked closer at the fancy invitation trapped behind the sun visor. Her slender fingers reached out and touched the fine paper, hesitant, almost awed.

"May I?" she asked. Unsure what she was thinking, he nodded.

Jess plucked the card from its spot and brushed her hands across the return address on the engraved invitation. A stallion was prominently embossed on the front.

"Ted Taylor," she breathed. "You know Ted Taylor."

Huh? Her voice was almost reverent.

"Yeah, that's my uncle." Seth gently pulled the invite from her fingers to glance at it. "I had forgotten this. He's throwing a big blowout tonight."

"You could help me!"

Seth found himself on the receiving end of a stunning smile. Jess leaned toward him, and he could practically smell her eagerness. For some reason his stomach tightened. He had the feeling he wasn't going to like what she suggested.

"I can't believe I let you talk me into this."

Jess grinned and rolled her eyes. That was the third time Seth had complained. He was smiling and shaking his head as he said it, though, so she decided he wasn't too upset with her. Plus, he was driving toward his uncle's house.

She couldn't get over the fact that she had never connected him with Ted Taylor. Ted Taylor owned the most renowned stable for breeding racehorses in this part of the country. He was an influential man who sat on various committees dealing with equine care and treatment. His passion was abused horses. Just as

Cody's had been. His endorsement could sway public opinion in her favor.

She shivered. On the other hand, a cold shoulder from him would convince many she and her brother were guilty. But she had to try.

And he was also well known for throwing lavish parties. Like this one. Parties where everyone brought an overnight bag because one day wasn't long enough to celebrate. Not to mention the fact that he lived almost an hour away from LaMar Pond on the outskirts of Spartansburg. Ted always opened the spring season up with a bang. Anyone who was anyone in the equestrian circle in northwestern Pennsylvania would be there. Breeders, coaches, trainers. All people who she and her brother had met in one capacity or another. It was possible that someone there might be able to provide some answers about what had really happened in the last few months of Cody's life.

"Are you sure you can spare this much time away from the stables?"

Seth was precious when he was concerned. *No way. Not going there.* Even if it was true, it would do no good for her to become attached. The butterflies currently fluttering in her stomach would go away if she ignored them. She cut a quick glance toward him and met melting brown eyes. Instead of going away the butterflies intensified.

What was the question? Oh, yeah.

"The stables will be fine. I texted my staff so they'll know to come in and take care of the morning chores. Even if I don't show up for a few days, the workers keep things moving. We keep charts on which animals need what to be done, so someone will be able to pick up the slack."

As the truck sloshed through the back roads toward Ted Taylor's party, she watched as the puddles on the road became progressively deeper. Rain continued to pound on the truck. The rhythmic swipe of the wipers could barely keep up. Her teeth tugged at her lower lip. Maybe convincing Seth to bring her to the party with him as his "plus one" hadn't been a great idea. With weather like this, they wouldn't be able to leave the party quickly or easily if she was treated badly by the other guests—which was a definite possibility. Many of them had treated her as if she had leprosy since Cody's death. Or as if she were a criminal. Which certainly accounted for the fact that she had not received an invite to this weekend's event for the first time in two years. Willa Taylor was a social snob.

Of course, it was also possible that one of them was responsible for the accidents. She shuddered and promised herself that if she saw a dark green sedan parked outside the ranch house, she'd have Seth take her home again. She cautioned herself against relying on him too heavily. She had struggled hard to prove herself to be a strong, independent woman. It wouldn't do to allow her former crush to gain too much leverage over her.

"This water is getting really deep," Seth stated, a frown pulling down the corners of his mouth. Outside, everything was gray. Gray clouds, gray sky, gray pools of liquid surrounding them as they drove. They went over the bridge. Jess looked down and felt a niggle of dread. The water was higher than she had ever seen it.

"There it is." Seth raised one hand to indicate the sprawling ranch ahead of them. His blinker flashed as he steered the truck into the long winding lane that served as the Taylor residence's driveway. The driveway was like the rest of Pennsylvania. It rose and dipped. It wasn't the smoothest ride, but Jess still released a sigh of relief that they'd finally arrived. It was followed by a shriek as Seth's tires hydroplaned. The back end of the pickup swerved to the right. Seth managed to get the vehicle back on track just in time to drive it through the next puddle. Only the puddle was more like a small pond. The motor sputtered and stalled. Stopped.

They were stuck at the ranch.

Seth tossed her a reassuring grin. "Don't worry. I'm sure we can find someone to help us get the truck started again. Or a lift back to town. It'll be fine."

She wasn't fooled. His grin was strained, and his jaw was tight.

Seth opened the door and splashed over to Jess's side to help her down. Grabbing her overnight bag with her fancy dress and toiletries safely tucked inside, she let Seth take her empty hand and jumped out. She landed with a muddy splash and grimaced. She was almost knee-deep in freezing water. Her cowboy boots would be trashed. Good thing she hadn't decided to wear the dress and heels in the truck. Seth shrugged out of his jacket and slung it over her shoulders. And shushed her when she started to protest. Giving in gracefully, she allowed Seth to grab her hand again and pull her up to the lane to the house. Standing beside Seth, she tensed as he raised his hand and jabbed the doorbell with his finger. Within seconds, the door swung open and their host came out to grab Seth in a bear hug.

Ted Taylor was an impressive-looking man in his mid-fifties. Now that she saw him and Seth side by side, she could see the resemblance in the shape of their faces and in the way they held themselves.

"Seth! So glad you could make it, son!" His booming voice made the voices inside the house grow silent. "So many people canceled because of the weather. You and your girlfriend will make an even dozen."

Jess forced herself to stand still and smile as he turned kind eyes to her. "It's good to see you again, Jess. I was very sorry to hear about your brother. Cody was a fine young man, and I for one have never doubted his integrity."

Blinking to clear her suddenly blurred vision, Jess cleared her throat. Even so, she knew her voice sounded more like a croak when she spoke. "Thank you, sir. It means a lot to hear that."

She stiffened her knees to cease their sudden trembling. If Ted believed in Cody's innocence, and hers, there was hope.

"What's she doing here?" an angry voice said.

Heat crawled up her face as Jess found herself the target of hostile stares. Apparently, Ted's faith in her wasn't universal. Well, she hadn't expected it would be. Yet. Resigned, she turned to face Ted's snobbish, socially conscious wife.

"Aunt Willa, this is my friend, Jess. My good friend." Her bruised heart warmed when Seth squeezed her hand.

Hardly a good friend. But she appreciated the show of support when those gathered glared.

"I'm surprised you would bring the likes of her into your family's house," his aunt said with a scornful sniff. "Or perhaps you saw a pretty face and didn't realize what kind of girl she was."

What kind of girl she was? Seriously?

"Actually, Jess and I go way back. Since high school."

Jess could just barely make out the sound of voices tumbling over each other. Yet even without hearing the words, she could tell by the frowns on their faces that the other guests were not pleased to have her in their midst. But none of that seemed to affect Seth. She read his lips and saw that he was basically telling his family that he believed in her and trusted her. Suspicion was nudged out of the way by shame and gratitude. Gratitude that God hadn't completely abandoned her. And shame that she was still harboring a grudge against Seth. Mortified, she remembered her bitter words in the truck. Was that really just a couple of hours ago?

"Seth, that girl's brother was..."

Ted shook his head at his wife. Sullenly, she quieted, but the baleful glint of her eyes let Jess know she was far from appeased. With false joviality, Ted pulled them into the house and began introducing them around. Jess found herself the recipient of several slights and sneers. It didn't help that her hearing aids amplified all the noise of music and voices to the same level. The harsh jumble of sound made separating individual voices out from the background ruckus impossible. She was forced to rely totally on lip reading. Soon her eyes grew strained and she felt a tension headache coming on. She understood enough to realize that the majority of the guests had felt in some way cheated or betrayed by her brother, and they were quite willing to transfer that anger to her, even though she wasn't deeply involved in the foundation. She should have been more invested. And maybe if she had been, she'd be more aware of what had occurred.

At one point, she looked over in the corner and saw a familiar face. Her brother's fiancée, Deborah, gave her a nod, but made no move to come over. She understood. Deborah had suffered enough. She had told Jess quite clearly after the funeral that she needed to put it all behind her. The man standing beside Deborah was familiar, too. Russ Breen, one of Ted's star trainers. She had heard that Deborah had attached herself to a new man. It seemed a little quick, and Jess's throat tightened seeing how rapidly Cody had been replaced in the other woman's life. It had only been a few months. She couldn't understand how someone could move on that easily.

She sure hadn't.

Seth tapped on her shoulder. Glancing over, she was surprised to see anger tightening the skin around his eyes. What had she done? Her own eyes widened when she realized that he was angry with the others, on her behalf. He lifted his hands and signed to her.

"We can't stay here. Let's get some help with the truck and go. I will help you find answers another way."

Glancing around, she swallowed. He was right. She wouldn't be able to get any answers here. She nodded at him.

Seth asked around to find out who could lend a hand with the truck. Soon they had a group of four men who agreed to help. She followed them outside and down the driveway. And gasped.

The truck was where they had left it. Water was up to the top of the wheels.

The bridge was gone.

Further investigation confirmed what she already suspected. All the roads were under water as a flash flood washed in. The ranch itself was safe on raised ground. But every path out of it was blocked.

Walking back into the house beside Seth, she folded her arms in front of her, rubbing her hands up and down them to bring some warmth back into her chilled body. The lights flickered, but thankfully stayed on. When she had suggested coming to the party with Seth, it had sounded like a good idea. She would have a chance to meet with people from the horse community and gauge their reactions. Maybe even be able to get some clue as to what had really happened. She had been so naive.

Ted walked back over to where she stood with Seth. He said something in a low voice that she wasn't able to catch. And he didn't move his lips much, so she couldn't read what he'd said. Seth angled his body and signed discreetly to her.

"Uncle Ted says our rooms are ready if we want to go up and rest or clean up a bit."

Translation: the other guests were not happy with her presence. And she understood that he felt it was better if they were moved away from the party. She wouldn't complain. The sooner she was away from the angry and disapproving stares, the easier she would feel. She walked up the stairs to her room ten minutes later, Seth behind her like he was guarding her back. Which, in a way, he was.

In the hallway, a man with a cowboy hat approached from the other side. There was something familiar about him. She had probably seen him at some horse event, but had never been introduced. Odd, because she knew most of the equestrian crowd in the area.

He never even glanced at her as he was passing. But instead, with a quick side step, he knocked her into the wall with his shoulder. Pain lanced through her as she hit the wall. He dashed down the steps.

"Hey!" Seth turned, clearly intending to give chase.

"No, please, Seth, I don't want to be up here by myself."

He hesitated, but nodded, a grim look around his mouth. She was fairly certain that he wasn't going give up. He'd be watching for that cowboy. And given his fantastic ability to recall details, he would be able to spot the man in an instant.

Outside her door, there was a copy of today's newspaper. On the front page was a picture of her barn, with a police car in the parking lot. The article was circled in red. Had the cowboy left it here? Was he the person responsible for the fire?

Her breath caught in her throat. She was trapped with a house full of hostile people. And one of them was out to get her.

THREE

Seth pushed open the door to the guest room assigned to Jess and stalked inside. The anger simmering inside him demanded action, but he had no outlet for it at the moment, other than making sure she was safe. Leaving no corner unchecked, he searched her room for any dangers, hidden or otherwise. It really burned him that someone had decided to play games with her. She was an innocent, no matter what her brother may have done. Or not done. Because right now, he was feeling like there was something other than revenge behind these attacks. Not that he could make that call. He wasn't a cop.

Speaking of calls, he pulled out his cell and glanced at it. Still no bars. He had tried to contact the police department on Ted's landline, but couldn't get through. He'd lived through enough flash floods and tornado warnings to know that the lines could get overwhelmed. Or that power lines in town could get knocked out easily enough. So now they were sitting ducks. Which meant that it was up to him to see that Jess was safe.

He needed to have a talk with his uncle about the dude in the hallway. His gut said the man wasn't the same person who had been following them earlier. Why act out in the open after being so secretive? But he was definitely a threat.

"Okay, Jess. I don't see anything," he declared after ten minutes. "I think you can go ahead and clean up. I'm going to go downstairs and grab us something to eat. Lock the door behind me. I think we should stay up here tonight, and then tomorrow see if we can find a way out of this mess."

She nodded, but didn't look comforted. Her mouth opened, then shut again. He waited.

"Do you think someone is just trying to scare me? Or am I really in danger?" Her hazel eyes glistened, but she didn't cry. He wouldn't have blamed her if she had. The urge to comfort her and tell her everything would be fine was strong. But even stronger was his need to be honest. His father had taught him how to deceive, and he resisted any semblance of similarity to that man.

"Jess, as much as I want to tell you no, I really think you're in trouble. Whoever this jerk is, we have to assume he's dangerous. He didn't hesitate to start a fire at the stables, did he?"

The last expression he expected to see cross her face was a smile. It was no more than a slight upward curling of her lips, but it was there. "What?"

She glanced down, heat staining her pale cheeks. "It's been a long time since I felt like someone was on my side, other than Rebecca and her family. Even the other workers at my stable aren't really people I feel I know. Cody hired them, not me."

That surprised him. "What about your parents?"

"You didn't know?"

"Know what?"

"My parents were killed in a car accident the summer I graduated from high school. My brother became my guardian."

Seth groaned. "He was all you had." Reaching out, he snagged her into a hug. She resisted for a second, then accepted the embrace, leaning against him. But only for an instant. When she started to pull away, he let her go.

"I wasn't alone, Seth. I had the Lord to lean on. And Rebecca's family was great. They have been checking on me constantly."

"What about the people at your church?" he asked. "Surely, you feel some sort of connection with them?"

Even her ponytail seemed to droop as she shook her head.

"No, not really." Furrows appeared on her forehead. She brought one hand up and rubbed at them, as if she could massage them away. "To be honest, I didn't give them much of a chance. At the funeral, I could see people staring at me, and couldn't deal with their pity. So I changed churches. I drive to Erie each Sunday and attend there where no one knows me. Well, except for Ernie. But he doesn't pry."

He blinked, but didn't ask any questions. He was anxious to move the conversation away from the topic of God. He had an itchy feeling whenever she mentioned her faith. There was even a brief moment when they arrived when he had been tempted to say a prayer. Just to see if it worked. Tempted. He didn't succumb. That didn't stop the feeling that he was on a slippery slope. There would be no point to it, he knew. His mother had trusted in God all her life. And she ended up cheated on and betrayed by her own husband. Not just once, but over and over. No, he was just fine as he was. God was okay for others, but he didn't see the need for himself.

But he was saddened to see Jess abandon her church community. His mother had found support in hers.

Jess tilted her head. Probably wondering where he had gone mentally.

The flickering lights reminded them both of their situation.

"I will be back." Seth retreated to the hall and pulled the door shut behind him. He waited until he heard the door lock click. Then he made his way down to the kitchen, hoping he wouldn't run into anyone along the way. Answering questions or fending snide comments about Jess was not high on his list of things he wanted to do. For the first time in his life, he found himself grateful that his uncle had inherited his family's taste for ostentation. The house he had built in the middle of nowhere, in addition to having enough bedrooms to rival a modest hotel, had two staircases leading down to the main level. Seth took the back stairs, which ended in a short hallway right outside the kitchen. Which was empty. His uncle had gone all out and had the event catered, so all the food and beverages were displayed in a fancy buffet line in the dining room. Music and laughter pounded in the air.

Efficiently, Seth put together some sandwiches and grabbed some bottles of water. He nabbed a couple pieces of fruit from a basket on the counter. Where did his aunt keep plastic bags? Opening the cupboard under the sink, he found one and stuffed the food inside.

Turning back to exit, he was dismayed to find he was no longer the sole occupant of the kitchen. The man standing in the doorway was watching him with cold eyes, a distinct sneer on his face. Great. First the man on the stairs, and now this guy. As far as Seth could recall, he had never seen him before. He was a bulky man, his beefy arms crossed over his barrel chest as he scowled at Seth.

Seth moved forward. He had done nothing wrong, and he was in his uncle's house. This man wasn't going to keep him from Jess.

"Where's your girlfriend, boy?" the man growled, an ugly edge to his rough voice.

"Excuse me." Seth made to move past the man. But the guy just wouldn't let him pass. Instead, he planted himself firmly in Seth's path.

"How dare you bring that little crook here? She and her brother cost me thousands of dollars. And a prize horse. Spreading tales about honest folk." Fury oozed from him. Quivering, he took a step toward Seth, nostrils flaring. Seth had no idea what the man was talking about. "I'll bet she's here to spread her brother's lies, isn't she? Thinks good ole Ted Taylor will be on her side? Well, I won't let her get the best of me again. She'd better watch who she messes with."

He probably expected Seth to back up. Seth wasn't about to give in. Instead, he took a step closer to him.

"You need to let me pass," Seth stated, keeping his voice low. "Whatever happened, it had nothing to do with Jess. And from what I know, you don't even have solid proof that it had anything to do with her brother, either." He took another step forward. And another. Satisfaction filled him when the man's eyes widened, confusion on his face. Seth managed to keep his expression and voice clear of all emotion. Years of dealing with his father had taught him that the best way to get a reaction was to show no emotion. "You don't want to do this. Not in my family's home."

The sneer returned to his opponent's face, although Seth noted he did step aside to allow Seth to move past. Still, he managed to get out one last taunt before Seth could walk away.

"I would be careful who I hung out with. She's going down." He swung around and stormed back toward the other guests. Seth watched him, filing away in his mind details about the man's appearance and what he said. That was definitely someone to keep a close eye on.

Carrying his cache of food, he returned back upstairs the same way he had come. He breathed easier when he arrived at Jess's room without further incident. He rapped sharply on the door, then grimaced. Deaf girl. Could she hear the knock? Maybe he should slide something under the door…

The door swung open, causing him to jump. Color flooded his face as she observed him, her eyebrows lifted, an amused expression on her face.

"Didn't you expect me to answer the door?" she queried.

"I wasn't sure if you could hear me knock."

Jess nodded, making her brown ponytail bounce. "It depends on how low the sound is."

A thought occurred to him. "We should have found a way to signal you, so you would know it was me."

When she shrugged and reached for the food, he recalled the meeting in the kitchen. Casually, trying not to seem too concerned so she wouldn't worry, he mentioned the confrontation and described the man.

A disturbed look came into her eyes. Lowering her chin, she sighed. He wished he could have waited before telling her something that so clearly upset her, but she needed to know. For her own protection.

"It sounds like Bob Harvey. He and his wife Lisa are very involved in breeding racehorses. They have been the loudest voices against us."

A sharp, sizzling sound made Seth jerk his head up. It was followed by a pop. A transformer had been blown. The room was pitched into darkness.

Jess froze. Her entire body grew tense.

She'd never told anyone, but she was afraid of the dark. And closed-in places. Had been ever since the incident in high school. A cold sweat covered her body as she remembered the feeling of cobwebs brushing against her skin. The musty smell of a wet mop sitting in a bucket of dirty water. The smell was so pungent, she could taste it on her tongue. Clenching her fists, she folded her arms across her chest and shoved her fists under them. She could still feel them shaking. The trembling spread to her legs.

Breathe, Jess. Breathe. Spiders are NOT crawling over you. You are not locked in a room. And you are not alone. Stranded for hours and hours. Getting colder...

No! She wouldn't think about that! She was a grown woman now. Surely she could get past this irrational fear. The fear that even now was holding her paralyzed. After a few deep breaths, she baby-stepped her way in the direction of the window, grunting as her shin knocked into something. At the window, she felt around until she located the cord to the blinds. Tugging on it, she sighed in relief as light drifted into the room. It pooled in the center of the room, leaving the edges in shadow. She shivered. Creepy.

Light? Where on Earth was light coming from? It was pouring outside. Glancing out the window, she saw a row of solar lights. The kind that only come on when it is dark outside. Ah. She hadn't noticed them before, probably because there had been other sources of light.

Seth stepped into the light, and she shivered again. For a very different reason.

"Jess, are you okay?"

She nodded. "Fine."

He folded his arms. Clearly she wasn't convincing enough.

"What do we do now?" she asked him. *Focus, Jess.* Yes, he's handsome and being kind. And yes, she was enjoying his company. But there was a maniac in this house waiting to get her and this power outage— whether accidental or deliberate—might give her attacker an opportunity. She needed to deal with that possibility. Attraction to Seth was a complication she couldn't afford.

"I'm not leaving you alone to deal with this tonight."

She shook her head, frowning. "You can't stay in my room. It wouldn't be right."

Did he just roll his eyes? Was he mocking her convictions? Drawing herself up to defend her beliefs, she paused when he raised his hands.

"I'm not suggesting that I stay in your room. But I do intend to camp outside your door."

Something soft and melty nudged her heart.

"But you need to rest, too," she argued. "Your room is just down the hall. You'd be close by if I needed you." It was a token protest at best. The idea of him going so far away in this hostile environment made her feel vulnerable.

Seth scoffed. "Like I'd rest in my own room? Sorry, Jess, but I'd be coming out to check on you every five minutes. There's no way I'd be able to sleep not knowing if you were safe."

The tension which had locked onto her neck loosened and rolled off her shoulders. He wasn't leaving her.

Jess squinted and looked at him. Really looked at him. His jaw was clenched and he was glaring at her. Like he was daring her to argue. A smile tugged at her mouth. He had no idea how unappealing the idea of staying here alone was. Deciding to let him think he'd won, she nodded. He nodded back. And although he didn't smile back at her, she sensed that her response had eased his belligerence.

"Good. Now that that issue is settled, I suggest we eat."

Gingerly, she lowered herself to sit cross-legged on the floor. Seth followed her example, then handed her a sandwich and a bottle of water. The darkness surrounding them made the room feel oddly intimate. Her cheeks grew warm, and she became aware of the subtle scent of his aftershave.

In complete silence they ate. The moment they were done, Seth excused himself to clean up. He made quick work of it, she was relieved to note. Then she scolded herself for being anxious just because he had left her side.

"I will be right outside the door," he promised. He used the flashlight app on his phone and pointed it so he could look around the room. What was he looking for? He strode to the desk and grabbed the plain wooden chair. Dragging it out into the hall, he placed it firmly in front of her door. She retreated back into the room. Even in the dim light, she could make out the bed. And if she remembered correctly…yes. There was an extra blanket on the end of it. Silently, she handed it to Seth. He smiled his thanks.

"Lock the door."

"Seth…"

She stopped when he shook his head. The weariness on his face tore at her, but she knew he wouldn't give in. One thing that she remembered clearly about Seth was that he had always been stubborn. It was no use trying to get him to change his mind. And frankly she was too tired to bother. Closing the door, she left him in hall—locking the door, as he'd ordered. Grabbing her bag, she changed into sweats and a T-shirt. With a prayer for their continued safety she moved into the room and lay down on the bed.

Turning on her side, she tried to get comfortable, but her hearing aid was pressed into the side of her head. It wasn't painful, but the sensation bothered her. Should she take the hearing aids off for the night? She always did when she went to sleep. It drained the batteries to wear them constantly. But she was almost completely deaf without them. At least with them, she could hear voices and environmental noises, even if she couldn't make out what was being said. When had she last changed the batteries? Was it really only this morning? Calculating, she figured even if she left them in tonight, she had another three days. And she had spare batteries in her overnight bag.

That settled it. They were staying in.

Flopping over onto her back, she sighed.

She didn't expect to fall asleep, but soon found herself drifting off.

She woke suddenly and bolted upright, heart pounding. Grabbing her phone, she checked the time. She had been asleep for two hours. What had wakened her? Sliding her legs over the side of her bed, she stood up and glanced around the room for some clue. Thunder rumbled and shook the house. The storm was directly overhead. That must have been what had startled her from sleep.

While she was relieved to have an explanation, she still felt anxious and unsettled. Rushing to the door, she opened it and peered out. Darkness enveloped everything. She knew the shadow in front of her was Seth, but dread filled her. She needed to see his face, to make sure he was safe.

"Seth?" she whispered. Her hand reached out and touched his face.

His phone light flashed on. He brought it closer to his face, probably so she could see his lips better. Standing, he stepped just inside her doorway.

"What's wrong?" he said, signing at the same time.

"I don't know. I just suddenly felt something was wrong."

He started to answer her, then abruptly stopped. His head swung around to the left, and he used his phone to peer into the darkness.

"What?"

He made a shushing motion. Bringing the phone close enough so she could see his hands again he signed, "I think someone might have just walked out of my room."

"Why didn't you notice them going into it?" she signed back.

"I fell asleep. The storm just woke me."

He stood up, every movement careful, and motioned that he was going to check his room. She grabbed his arm. Was he crazy, going after some maniac by himself? Using his phone for light again, he signed. "We are trapped. We'll be safer once we know. Wait for me in your room."

She wasn't so confident that confronting her attacker would make them any safer, but it did make sense to figure out who they were dealing with. But as for waiting for him in her room... She looked back into the dark cavern beyond her doorway. Uh-uh.

Decision made, she stepped out into the hallway and started to follow him. A frown crossed his face. But he didn't argue.

They crept to his room, but didn't enter. He pointed toward the stairs and signed. She nodded to show she understood. Someone was arguing downstairs. Possibly whoever had left his room. She needed to keep close. He began to creep down the stairs, his steps exaggerated. For a second, she hesitated. She could make out the sounds of muffled voices below. The voices were too low and garbled for her to decipher much more than that. There were at least two voices, but she couldn't even tell what gender they were.

Seth was getting ahead of her. She watched his shadow creep down another step. She went after him, using her hands to guide her along the wall. Fortunately, there was enough light coming in from the windows on the outside wall that she could make out the outline of the steps. She took care to step as gently as she could, fighting panic, knowing she wouldn't hear it if the stairs creaked. But whoever was at the bottom of the stairs would.

The hair on the back of her neck stood on end. Without knowing why, Jess knew something was wrong.

A hand grabbed her shoulder. Jess jumped, starting to turn. For a brief instant, she was aware of a slight aroma that she could not quite place. A second hand touched her back. A single hard shove propelled her toward the edge of the stairs. A scream ripped from her throat as she crashed downward into the darkness.

FOUR

Air whooshed past her ears as she fell, tumbling into the darkness. She pitched forward, flailing her arms, desperate to catch the railing, or anything that might break her fall. Her fist clipped something.

Seth's chin.

He must have turned toward her. She landed against him.

Unfortunately, instead of stopping her fall, he was knocked off balance, as well. His arms closed around her, and even in her terror she realized he was trying to shield her as they continued crashing down the stairs.

But the crashing thankfully only lasted for another second.

Their downward spiral came to an abrupt halt. Seth's whole body shuddered as his back slammed against the wall on the landing. Inertia had her thudding hard against his chest.

"Oof!" Seth's breath puffed against her ear. His arms tightened around her. Lying so close to him, she could feel both their hearts racing. Briefly, she dipped her head and pressed her forehead to his chest.

They were alive. Someone had deliberately pushed

her down the stairs, but they had survived. But for how long? It wasn't likely that whoever had pushed her was going to give up. On the contrary, the attacks were escalating.

Why had the person chosen to show their hand, here? Did they think the hostile environment would leave her so vulnerable that no one would notice, would assist her?

Gratitude welled in her heart. Because she wasn't alone. God had sent her Seth. An unlikely hero, given their past, but who was she to question the ways of the Almighty?

Carefully, she pushed away from Seth. He stood, then gave her a hand to help her up. The arguing they had heard moments before was gone. She could hear doors around them slamming, felt the vibrations on the landing of someone moving up the stairs toward them. She tensed. Seth's arms moved again, this time to shove her behind him.

A wide beam of light cut through the dark, moving in a back and forth pattern as someone approached. It came to land on them and Jess could see that it came from a heavy-duty LED flashlight.

"Seth? Jess? What's going on?" Ted exclaimed, his loud voice echoing in the stairway. "I thought I heard someone screaming."

"It's okay, Ted. Jess—"

"I just tripped on the stairs," she interrupted Seth. He had no clue that she had been pushed, and she didn't want to get into it now, not when everyone else was closing in. For now, she just wanted to hurry and move to a new location. Already the top of the staircase and the landing below were filling with other guests, their flashlights aimed straight at them. And although she couldn't see their faces clearly, she imagined many of them were filled with anger at being awakened. Or maybe even malicious joy that she had suffered a mishap.

"Probably stumbling under the weight of all that guilt," a familiar voice called out. Bob Harvey. Jess kept herself from reacting, although she could do nothing about the anxiety crawling like ants over her skin.

Seth put a hand on her shoulder, then leaned over and whispered something in his uncle's ear. Ted started. She literally saw the beam of light from his flashlight jump.

"It's okay, folks," their host called back in an overly jovial voice. Was she the only one who could tell how forced his tone was? "Go on back to bed. I'm sure all will be set to rights in the morning."

Meaning the electricity would be back on and the flood waters would recede, she supposed. One could only hope.

Seth, keeping her at his back, moved slightly away from her. She shivered. It had gotten colder. Or at least that's how it felt without his warmth nearby.

She kept her eyes focused on Ted and Seth as the other guests meandered back to their rooms, taking their flashlights with them. Amazing how long it took people to walk a few feet. After the last door had closed, Ted nodded and jerked his head, indicating they were to follow him.

Jess was startled when a hand closed over hers. Seth had reached back to take her hand. Tears stung the back of her eyes at his silent care. Rapidly, she blinked them away, chastising herself for giving in to irrational emotions. Of course he took her hand. He was just being a gentleman, making sure she didn't fall again.

Whatever. She was still touched by his actions.

Ted led them into a room on the other side of the house. Even with the high-powered flashlight, she still managed to bang her shins on objects twice. Tomorrow she was sure to have bruises to remember this fun evening by. Upon entering the room, she was pleased to note a fireplace with a roaring blaze. There were three candles flickering on tables. It was a relief to be in a room that was warm and reasonably well lit.

Ted turned off his light, then swiveled to shut and lock the door. When he faced them again, his normally cheerful face was more serious than she could ever recall seeing it before. The direness of their situation stabbed at her.

"Okay, son, want to tell me what this is about?"

Seth glanced over and met her eyes. She understood what he was asking. Slowly, she nodded, hoping she was making the right decision. Her instincts said to trust Ted; that he was on her side. But she knew it was very possible he was only being a good host. Or worse. Yet either way, what choice did she have, really? She was stuck in his house until they could find a way out of this mess.

"Do you need me to sign?" Seth asked her.

Again, she was surprised by his thoughtfulness. The longer she was around him, the more she felt sure he had truly changed.

"No. It's quiet, so I can hear you pretty well. And there's enough light for me to read lips, if necessary. Thanks for checking."

He nodded, then got down to business.

"Someone is after Jess, Uncle Ted." Seth began. "Even before we arrived here, we had the feeling someone was trying to hurt her, but since yesterday, things have escalated." Seth explained about the cowboy in the hallway, and the intruder in his room. He even mentioned his confrontation in the kitchen with Bob Harvey. At that, anger crossed Ted's affable face. Even in the less than perfect light, she could see the angry tide of red rolling up his neck.

"I should have known that hothead would cause trouble. But to confront my own nephew in my house? Why, I have half a mind to—"

"There's something else you should know." Jess hated to butt in, but she knew she needed to say something before her courage deserted her. Or before he got off on a tangent, which Ted was well-known for doing.

Both men turned to face her. Seth's eyebrows raised in surprise.

"I didn't fall down those steps. I was pushed."

Complete.

Silence.

Jess swallowed, the reality of her situation crashing down on her as she said the words out loud. Her shoulder and back tingled where her attacker had touched her. "Someone pushed me." Just saying the words made the fear and shock rise again, even worse than before. "I'm going to be sick!"

Her stomach rebelled, and she had to focus all her attention on keeping the contents of their late supper down. She retched, but thankfully nothing came up. Still, she had a nasty taste in her mouth.

An arm came around her shoulders. Seth.

"Easy, Jess. It's the shock. You're safe. I'm here. If you need to be sick, that's okay. I'll take care of you."

"I'm good," she whispered, suddenly drained. "Just want to sit down."

Seth led her over to the recliner positioned next to the fireplace. Ignoring her protests, he helped her to sit down, than covered her with the afghan from the couch. She felt like such a baby, being fussed over.

"Jessica, are you sure someone pushed you? You couldn't have fallen?" Looking into Ted's anxious face, she wished with all her heart she could tell him that she could have been mistaken. But she knew what she had felt.

"I'm sorry, Ted. I felt someone shove me. There was no way I fell."

Seth knelt down beside the chair, his face pinched and concerned.

"Did you happen to get a look at who it was? If it was a man or a woman?"

"No, I'm sorry. It happened so quickly."

Ted paced for a moment. Then he came to stand in front of them, his large hands fisted on his hips. "We need to call the police!"

Seth sighed, scrubbing his hands over his face. He dropped them, and shook his head. "I agree, but how? The cell service here is nonexistent. Is your landline functional?"

Crossing the room with long strides, Ted picked up the wireless phone sitting on the end table. He pushed a button and listened for a moment. Shoulders drooping, he set it back down. "No dial tone. Don't know if it's the lines or if the battery is drained. This phone has been spotty for the past few weeks."

"So we're stuck." Jess stated the obvious.

"We're stuck," Seth repeated, pounding his fist on his thigh. "The question is who here could be out to get you?"

Jess snorted. Seth looked at her, eyebrows raised.

"Sorry, but I mean, who isn't?" she said. "You saw that crowd. Honestly, Seth, even your aunt treated me like so much garbage."

Oops. That was probably not the right thing to say. Both Seth and Ted stiffened. Then Ted relaxed and rubbed the back of his neck. A tired chuckle rumbled from his mouth. Surprised, Jess looked at him.

"Yeah, my Willa can come on strong. But she has a heart of gold. You'll have to trust me on this one."

She wasn't so sure, but decided now was not the time to anger their one ally.

Turning the conversation in a different direction, she asked, "What about the car?"

Ted shook his head. "Car? What car?"

"I've been followed by a green sedan."

Even before she finished, he was shaking his head again. "Little lady, in case you haven't noticed, this is pickup country. No self-respecting person in this house would dare to drive any vehicle that wasn't fit to tow a horse trailer."

Well, there was that. Now what?

Ted turned to his silent nephew. Silent, but those deep eyes were alert. If she could read his mind, she was pretty sure he was storing up every nuance, every word being said to dissect later.

"I don't think y'all should go back to your rooms tonight, Seth."

Ted's pronouncement had both their heads turning to face him in surprise. And if Jess was being honest, she was relieved, too. Down here near the fire seemed a whole lot safer than upstairs in her quiet room, nestled so near those who wished her miles away. Or dead.

"Where should we stay?" Seth asked, his air cautious.

"Right here. The door is locked. There's a fire. And you and I can take turns keeping watch. Then in the morning we can come up with a plan. Things always look brighter when the sun's up."

"What about Aunt Willa?"

Ted snorted. "Your aunt is sound asleep. She won't even notice that I'm not there until morning. And I'm always up by five to take care of the horses, anyway. She never stirs before eight."

Jess felt her clenched muscles relax bit by bit as he spoke.

Morning. She just had to hang on until morning.

Could they hang tight until morning?

She claimed someone had pushed her. If he hadn't been in front of her to protect her from the worst of the fall, or if the stairwell had been a straight drop without that landing... Anger flooded his once logical mind. Here, in his uncle's house, she was being stalked and attacked. He had let her down so long ago. This time, he was resolved to redeem himself. He would keep her safe, no matter what. Seth was no cop, but he was a grown man, and he was fit.

He would stand between her and any dangers.

Maybe a prayer wouldn't hurt?

He shook his head, ridding himself of the thought. God had stopped listening to him years ago.

Ted moved with his lumbering gait toward the door, his flashlight once again in his large hand. "I'm going to go get some extra bedding from the linen closet. Lock the door behind me. I'll call out to you when I come back so you'll know it's me. If anyone else knocks, well, just let 'em stew. Don't even acknowledge it."

As if. Seth merely nodded. Rising, he followed Ted to the door, locking it securely behind his uncle. He listened to the familiar heavy footsteps fading. What now? Peeking over at Jess, he frowned. With the poor lighting, it was hard to tell, but he was sure she looked pale. And why not? The poor woman had already had enough hurled at her to wear anyone down. She needed to rest.

He moved in front of her, squatting so they were eye to eye. Her gaze was steady. Good, even if she was scared, which he knew she had to be, she wasn't allowing it to control her. His respect for her rose a notch.

"Jess, why don't you try to get some rest?" he suggested. "Tomorrow's gonna be a hard day, and you'll need to be able to keep on your toes."

Her head tilted, causing her hair to tumble over her shoulder. When had she removed her ponytail? He had the sudden urge to brush the caramel-colored strands back, just to see if they were as soft as they looked.

Yeah. Like that was an appropriate thought to be having right now. *Use your head, Seth. Even if you weren't in a dangerous situation, there's no way someone like her would want to be with someone like you.* That thought brought him up short. He wasn't a man who could do relationships. There was too much of a risk that he would harm the woman he was seeing, unthinkingly.

"What about you?" her soft voice, slightly slurred with exhaustion, reminded him of his question.

"You heard my uncle. He and I will take turns. And I will sleep while he has the watch." Something occurred to him. "You did hear him, right?"

The barest hint of a smile teased him. "Yes. I heard him. Although, if you and he are both here with me, maybe I can take out my hearing aids? Save the batteries? I don't want to have to use the spares I brought until I have to. Who knows how long we'll be out here."

Hopefully not long.

"Go ahead."

Reassured, she reached up and removed her hearing aids. He watched as she opened the battery doors to turn them off, and set them on the end table beside the chair. Hearing Ted's voice outside the door, he hurried over and let his uncle in. Ted passed out blankets, then sat down in the rocking chair near the door.

"Jess. Jess?" No answer. She couldn't hear him, and her eyes were closed. Was she asleep already? Unbelievable. He could never fall asleep that quickly.

"I'll take first watch, Seth."

He nodded at his uncle, then looked at the couch. It went against the grain for him to lie down while she was in the chair. But Jess was curled up on the only other possible spot in the room—and if she was already asleep then he certainly wasn't going to wake her up to move her. Reluctantly, he lay down.

"Wake me in a couple of hours?" he asked his uncle.

"Yep. You just get some sleep, son. Mornin' will be here before you know it."

* * *

Seth came awake slowly. He stretched, frowning. Man, he had the worst crick in his neck. Suddenly, the memories of what had happened before he fell asleep flooded his mind. He shot up on the couch, knocking the fluffy little pillow he had been using on the floor. His eyes flew to the clock. It was almost five in the morning.

His uncle was sitting in his chair, rocking slightly as he watched his nephew.

"Why didn't you wake me?"

"Seemed a shame…you were both sleeping so soundly. And I figured you would need to stay on your toes later. We both will."

"Electric still off?"

"Yep. Got some emergency generators that kicked on, but that's about it. Landline's still down. I'm getting one bar on my cell phone—doubt it's enough for a call to go through, though." The older man stood with a groan, putting his hand on his back. "You're awake now. I'm going to go take care of the horses."

The older man left. When he returned forty-five minutes later, he had a couple more flashlights. Seth excused himself to go to his room. While he had the opportunity, and before the other guests stirred, he wanted to go through his things and see if he could find what last night's intruder was after.

The house was still dark. He tightened his grip on the flashlight he had borrowed. Arriving at his room, he cautiously pushed the door open. Whoever had been in there hadn't shut it the whole way. Probably didn't want the noise to awaken Seth from his perch outside Jess's room. The hair prickled on his neck as he entered the room. What could they have been searching for? Nothing seemed to be out of place. His duffel bag was still sitting on the chair next to the bed. But wait…was it unzipped? Yeah, it was—and he was sure he hadn't left it that way. He quickly emptied the contents on the bed, holding the light between his chin and chest. He couldn't see that anything was missing.

Shoving everything back in his bag, he scowled. So what were they looking for?

Unless…

Unless they weren't sure which room was his. The thought curdled his blood. If they had been searching for Jess's room, what were they planning to do if they'd found her?

Seth shuddered, and forced his mind back to the present. He couldn't afford to let the "what ifs" get control.

Head full of questions, Seth left the room and headed back down to join Jess. As soon as it was light out, they'd start looking for a way out of here.

Passing her room, he paused. Listened. Someone was in there. And from the sound of it, they were searching for something with a vengeance. Holding his breath, he stepped closer to the door and gently turned the knob.

Paused.

Waiting.

The sound of things being moved around inside continued. Whoever was inside hadn't heard him.

I should go get Ted, he thought to himself. That was clearly the intelligent thing to do. Except that any movement away from the door might alert whomever was inside. And what if the intruder was finished and left the room before he returned? They might miss the chance to find out who Jess's attacker was. He couldn't let the opportunity to stop this nut case pass him by.

The blood was roaring in his ears as he carefully opened the door and stepped inside the room.

The first strains of morning coming in the window highlighted the contents of Jess's overnight bag strewn all over the floor, her toiletries everywhere. A large hulking figure stood over her bag, systematically pulling items out one at a time.

That was it. Seeing the man's hands on Jess's personal items was the last straw.

At Seth's entrance, the man dropped the bag and charged at Seth. Seth backed up against the door for more room, and swung the flashlight. Thwack! With a grunt, the man stopped. But only for a second. Before Seth could call for help, the man was upon him, trying to get his hands at Seth's throat.

Falling back on the moves he'd learned during his days on the high school wrestling team, Seth twisted away and dove for his attacker's knees. Using his weight, he pushed the man off balance. Where his attacker had breadth and pounds on Seth, Seth had agility and years of weight training behind him.

The larger man managed to get an elbow into Seth's windpipe, but it gave Seth the opening he needed to hook the man's arm with his, forcing it back. Using his legs as leverage, he forced the man over, the one arm twisted at an impossible angle. The man's breath started to come out in wheezing gasps.

Suddenly, a bright light shone upon the two on the floor.

"Seth! What are you doing? Bob? Is that you?"

Ted moved into the room.

Seth let Bob Harvey go and stood next to his uncle, keeping his glare fixed on Bob.

"He was going through Jess's things. I'm guessing he's her attacker."

Bob's head jolted up. The sneer melted off his face. "Hey! I never attacked your girl."

Seth clenched his fists. It would feel so good to slug the dude. But it would solve nothing. "Then what were you doing? This—" he swept his arm out, indicating the mess Bob had made "—doesn't exactly look like innocent behavior."

An angry flush stole up the man's thick neck. Any second, steam would pour from his ears. "I told you, her brother was spinning stories about me before he killed himself. I'm aiming to see if she's planning on messing with my rep."

As far as excuses went, it was pretty weak.

Seth started to scoff, then realized something. If Ted was here, then Jess was...

"Ted! What are you doing up here? Where's Jess?"

"I got a text from you that you had the intruder and needed my help."

Alarm bells went off in his head. "I never sent any texts."

Reaching into his back pocket, he found just what he was expecting to find. Nothing. His cell phone was gone. The last time he had had it was last night on the stairs.

"My phone's gone! I dropped it last night when I tried to catch Jess. Someone must have picked it up."

Ted cast a threatening look at Bob.

Heart sinking, Seth knew they had a problem. "It wasn't him, Ted. He was in here searching her room when that text must have been sent. And he had no idea I was with him until I burst in on him."

The uncle and nephew looked at each other, horror dawning on both their expressions.

"Jess!"

FIVE

Where was Seth?

Jess put her hearing aids in and glanced at the clock on the wall. Ted had only been gone for a few minutes. She thought back to the text Ted had received. Why had Seth specifically said he needed her to stay where she was? Why wasn't it safe for her to accompany the older man?

Her phone vibrated in her back pocket. Finally! Grabbing the phone, she swiftly swiped her finger across the screen to unlock it and access the text.

The number was unfamiliar.

This is Seth. Situation under control. I need you to meet me by the back door.

Did she ever give Seth her number? She couldn't recall, although maybe he got it from Ted. His uncle was listed under her business contacts. But it would have made more sense for Ted to have sent the text. Unless Ted was busy with whatever they were doing?

She shrugged, trying to rid herself of the prickly unease dancing over her skin. Every instinct was screaming for her to stay where she was. She pulled her bottom lip in between her teeth and gnawed at it gently while she juggled her choices. She could, of course, remain in the room near the warm fire. That seemed the sensible thing to do. But what if Seth honestly did need her? She hated to think of him waiting for her. Especially if he had found something important. But why couldn't he have just said so? Maybe he was afraid someone else would see the text.

Whatever. How much could it hurt just to go to the door and look out? Maybe if someone friendly, like Ted or even Deborah, came by, she could ask them to go with her.

Replacing her phone, she got to her feet and strode to the door with the intention of just sticking her head out and peeking down the hallway. Instead, she opened the door and came face to face with Willa Taylor. So much for Ted's declaration that Willa wouldn't awaken before eight. Seeing the frozen sneer on the lady of the house's face silenced any hesitation ringing in her head. She couldn't remain in the same room as Willa.

Not giving the lady the time to say anything snide, Jess ducked past her and into the hall. She couldn't resist turning her head to look over her shoulder. And grimaced. Willa had marched straight into the room and was dramatically spraying disinfectant over the slept-on furniture.

Ouch.

Jess hurried on to the kitchen. She slowed her pace as she heard voices coming from the living room. She definitely didn't want to run into anyone else. Not in this hostile environment. Tucking herself in against the wall, she peeked around the corner. The cowboy she had met on the stairs was in the room, talking to Lisa Harvey.

Whipping her head back before they saw her, Jess struggled to control her breathing. Again, she doubted her wisdom in coming to find Seth. She should have just sent a text back telling him to come and get her. Now she was stuck. She couldn't go back to the parlor where she'd spent the night, not with Willa prowling around in there. And she couldn't stay here, out in the open.

Sucking in a deep breath to calm her nerves, she muttered a prayer under her breath. Then, she gathered up her courage and peered around the corner again. A sigh of relief slipped from her. Cowboy and Lisa Harvey were heading out the front door. A few moments later, she spotted Lisa out the window, heading away from the house.

Now was her chance.

Staying close to the walls, Jess continued on to the large kitchen.

To her dismay, she found the room empty.

Seth was nowhere in sight.

Doubt whispered to her again. Maybe it hadn't been Seth sending the text. She should have followed her gut and stayed locked in the parlor, safe and out of sight. Too late now. Most likely, one of the other guests was holding him up. Maybe even trying to question him about her.

She shuddered.

Surely he would understand if she sent him a text telling him to meet her somewhere else. Somewhere more secure, where she wouldn't feel so vulnerable and out in the open. Decision made, Jess started to turn. The aroma she'd smelled on the stairs tickled her nose right before an arm wrapped tight around her neck. She couldn't breathe!

Clawing at the arm, she kicked her legs and fought to pry the arm off her windpipe. Spots danced in front of her eyes.

A burning sensation bit into the tender skin on the side of her neck. Her vision blurred.

Even as she struggled, a heavy, weighted feeling slid through her.

She was going down.

It was freezing.

Why was she on the floor? Pressing her palms against the smooth surface—concrete?—Jess pushed herself to her hands and knees. A rush of dizziness threatened to send her toppling. She bowed her head and waited for the wave to pass.

Steady now, she slowly gained her feet. Wherever she was, it was pitch dark.

A whimper crawled up her throat. She bit her lips to keep it inside. She shuddered, and knew only a fraction of it was from the cold.

Had she slept through the day? That hardly seemed likely. Something had happened...

The memory of her struggle with her attacker slammed into her, robbing her breath. She could still feel that arm around her throat. And the burning sensation in her neck. Reaching up, she touched one cold finger to her neck, wincing at the tender spot covered in something crusty. Blood. She must have bled when the person jabbed her with whatever it was they used. She slipped her left hand to her back pocket, reaching for her phone. Her jeans were icy and stiff. For the first time she realized that her back was wet. And apparently covered with mud. She pushed her frozen fingers under the mud, and was unsurprised to discover her pocket was empty. Her phone was gone. She really hadn't expected her attacker to leave it on her.

The dark pressed in on her. The silence surrounded her like thick cotton. One hearing aid was missing, the other was weak.

Okay, Jess. Okay. Think. Don't panic. Seth is going to be looking for you.

But what if he wasn't? What if he was trapped, too?

This line of thought was helping no one. *Please, Lord, help me. And please let Seth be okay.*

She needed to figure out where she was. She held her arms out to start feeling her way around the space, shivering at the cold air swirling around her. Her jaw was starting to ache. Her teeth had never chattered so hard in her life.

Taking a small step forward, her left hand bumped into something. Something cold. Hard. It was large, and swung slightly.

Horror dripped down her spine as a suspicion began to grow in her mind. She blocked it. She had to be mistaken. Until her right hand bumped a second one.

She was in the slaughterhouse freezer.

She knew Ted ran a slaughterhouse on his property as a second business. Many of the Amish in the area used his services since he was so close.

What she couldn't figure out was why she was in it.

There was a high probability that she wouldn't be found until the flood waters receded. Which could be days. No one was going to coming to pick up their meat or drop off new orders before then.

Every instinct in her urged her to scream. She was stuck in a cold, dark, small enclosed area. Images of dying here popped into her head. She squeezed her eyes shut and focused on breathing normally. Forcing panic aside, she turned her body and felt for the door. Her fingers were tingling. Was she getting frostbite?

Ignoring her physical distress, she bumped around the cold freezer, her movements growing clumsier as the cold started to take its toll. She no longer noticed her aching jaw.

Finally, after what seemed like an eternity, she bumped into the door. It wouldn't budge. Locked. Or blocked. It didn't matter which.

Banging her fists against the door, she screamed. Pain shot through her hands. Her wrists. Up her arms and into her shoulders. She kept banging as the air became thin. The walls...she couldn't see them, but they were closing in on her. Something crawled across her skull. A spider? Panic gained control.

"Help! Help me! I'm stuck in the freezer!"

She yelled until her throat became raw. She leaned her head against the door. It was no use. Who was going to hear her out here? Everyone else was safe inside the warm house. Weariness melted into her bones. Wait... when had her eyes closed?

Dragging them open, she blinked. It was so hard to keep them open, but she continued to struggle to do just that. After a while, she forgot why it was so important. She was so tired. All she wanted was to rest. Leaning against the freezer door she gave in and let her eyes close. Just for a minute. All she needed was a short nap.

Her legs seemed to lose strength. Weariness weighed her down. The door was smooth against her cheek as she allowed herself to slide down. Down, down, down until she was sitting on the floor.

Dropping her hands to her lap, she let her head fall forward. Her chin touched her chest.

There was something she needed to do, but whatever it was eluded her.

Something about Seth?

She'd worry about it later. She was so sleepy. Needed... nap...

Seth dashed down the stairs, his uncle hot on his heels. Tearing through the house, he ignored the few guests who dove out of his way, muttering in displeasure. He arrived in the parlor to find his aunt inside. Jess was nowhere to be seen.

Where was she? Every fiber of his body screamed at him that she was in danger.

One thought darted across his brain, standing out.

I should pray. Jess would want me to pray.

The impulse was an uncomfortable one, and his inclination was to ignore it. But he couldn't shake the feeling that Jess would want him to pray. And if he was the one missing, she would no doubt pray for him.

Lord, protect her.

Was that enough? He hoped so.

"Aunt Willa, where's Jess?"

His aunt faced him, her lips pinched and eyes narrowed. He winced. He hadn't meant to raise his voice to her.

"Please, it's really important."

She sniffed. "I came in just after she snuck out of here. No telling what she was up to."

Calm. Stay calm. "Any idea where she was headed?"

"Well, I didn't actually stop to talk with her. She could have tried to swim home for all I care… Hey! Seth Travis! Come back here!"

Seth ignored her voice, shrieking after him. He dashed out the door, nearly colliding with his uncle.

"She's not here. We have to find her."

To his credit, Ted didn't stop to ask time-wasting questions. Although Seth did note that he tossed an angry glare toward his wife. The two men began to search the house inch by inch. Unsurprisingly, no one was willing to admit that they had seen Jess. Over an hour later, he met his uncle again in the kitchen.

He stopped in the doorway. Jess wasn't in the room. He hadn't really expected to find her there, he admitted to himself. His eyes scanned the room. And stopped. He crouched down. There, a couple of feet away from the door, lay a Behind-the-Ear, or BTE hearing aid. He had missed it the first time through. It was half hidden by the welcome mat. He reached out one hand and picked it up, bringing it close to inspect it.

"What is it, son?"

Seth looked into Ted's concerned face. Flicking his eyes behind the older man, he could see a group of the other guests gathered there. His mouth tightened when he saw Bob Harvey amongst them.

"It's Jess's hearing aid," he answered his uncle. His uncle's face paled. "It's broken. I'd say someone stepped on it."

Willa entered the room. The haughty expression she normally wore had been replaced by confusion. "She left her hearing aid in the kitchen?"

Shaking his head, Seth stood and walked to the back door. "No. She would never go without her aid. She's completely deaf without them. Something happened to her."

Why had he left her alone? Noticing that his fingers were trembling slightly, he closed them around the fractured hearing aid. The shattered plastic scratched his palm. He felt it all the way to his heart.

Ignoring the burst of chatter that broke out, he walked outside. And sucked in a breath.

Amidst the rain-soaked muck that was out the back door, a clear path had been left by something being dragged. Something that was big enough to be a human body. All the moisture in his mouth instantaneously dried up. The path was narrow and straight enough that he doubted the person being dragged had been conscious enough to struggle. And, knowing that person was Jess, he rushed outside, regardless of the rain pelting his head, molding his hair to his scalp and running mercilessly into his eyes.

None of that mattered. Neither did the clomping feet behind him.

Except...

"First-aid kit!" he barked at his uncle.

Ted nodded once before pivoting mid-step and rushing back toward the house.

The path wound around the side of the house. Seth quickened his pace, gritting his teeth in frustration when he was forced to slow down or risk slipping and falling flat on his face.

The path led to the front of his uncle's slaughterhouse. Ripping open the front door, he saw immediately that the path continued. The scant light from the cloudy skies was enough for him to see inside the building. His uncle reappeared just as he entered.

"Open the blinds!" Ted yelled. He and another guest went from window to window, pulling up the blinds to let the morning light filter inside.

Seth stopped in front of a large metal door, horrified. He knew from memory that the door in front of him was to the walk-in freezer. Granted, there was no electricity right now, but there was enough frozen food in that freezer to keep it artic for days.

Shoving the latch aside with fingers that shook, he pulled the huge door open.

And caught Jess as she toppled out.

Her face was white, tinged with blue. The back of her head and body was covered with a thick coat of crusty, frozen mud.

Gently, he picked her up and carried her into the main room. As he held her close, he glanced down, and nearly lost his composure at the sight of the blood dried on the side of her throat. Swallowing the rage that vibrated in his gut, he laid her down on the floor as if she was made of porcelain.

And then he set about doing what he did best. For the first time in his life, he wondered if God had put the desire to be a paramedic in his heart for this moment. Ridiculous. He drew upon his training to focus all his thoughts, all his energies, on his patient. Now was not the time for philosophizing. Or for letting worry for the lovely, deathly pale woman at his feet distract him. *Box up your emotions and ship 'em out, Seth.*

The well-known mantra calmed him.

First thing first, check her vitals.

She was breathing, and had a steady pulse. Check.

Now, to get her warm.

Someone shuffled too close to him, hampering his movements.

"Get back!" he ordered, barely recognizing the harsh voice as his own.

"Seth," his aunt quavered, wringing her hands. Her normally haughty expression was edging on frantic, her voice whiny. "I'm sure this was an accident. No one here would…"

"Get. Out. Of. My. Way." He bit off each word, all but snarling at the woman beside him.

Willa jumped away, her expression an odd combination of dismay and affront. He'd worry about smoothing her feathers later. Maybe. Right now, Jess was all that mattered.

Efficiently, he called for blankets and clean clothes. Within minutes, Jess was in dry clothes and bundled in blankets, her feet elevated.

He monitored her closely, relieved to note her color was returning. She was beginning to stir.

"Jess? Jess? Can you hear me?" He raised his voice. A thought occurred to him. Gently, he reached over and removed her other hearing aid. Cupping his hand over the small microphone, he lifted it close to his ear, listening for feedback. But there was no whistling. The tiny battery was dead, drained by the frigid temperature. Or possibly the device itself had been damaged by being slogged through the wet, muddy terrain.

But Jess was alive.

"Why isn't she answering?"

He sighed as his aunt's anxious voice reached his ears. Now that the immediate danger was past, he'd have to deal with her.

"She's still unconscious. And without her aids, she can't hear me calling."

Hearing the sharpness in his tone, he sucked in a deep breath of cold, Pennsylvania air to calm himself. None of this was his aunt's fault. But really, the woman needed to take it down a notch. She was family, but he was this close to publicly disowning her.

Okay, not really.

Whispers distracted him. Glancing behind her, he grimaced. At least six other people were standing behind the Taylors. Great. He had an audience to witness the drama unfolding.

Before he could say anything to the nosy, judgmental crowd, Jess moaned. Immediately the conversation ceased. Seth switched back into paramedic mode and began taking stock of her condition, watching her for any signs of injury or disorientation.

With a flutter, her eyes opened. His breath left him with a whoosh as he saw the confused, but alert, expression in the hazel depths.

"Seth?" As she said his name, her eyes widened. "I can't hear."

A panicked expression crossed her face as she moved under the blankets. He understood. She wanted to free her hands to check on her hearing aids. He reached out and touched her shoulder. She stilled, her eyes seeking his.

"Your left aid was on the kitchen floor, smashed," he told her grimly, signing and speaking at the same time. "The right one isn't working, either. I suspect that the battery is dead, but it could have water damage."

"Water damage?"

"You were dragged outside through the rain." Fury

rose up in him. For a second, he couldn't breathe through the anger choking him. He had never understood the phrase "seeing red." Now he did. When he could talk again, he continued. "They left you in the freezer."

The color that had so recently filled her pretty face drained out again.

"Someone attacked me in the kitchen. I was looking for you. You sent me a text…"

Her voice dwindled as he shook his head slowly. Someone was going to pay for this.

"I never sent a text. My phone is gone." He cast a fierce glance at the crowd behind him. "Someone took it."

"Seth, look what I found in the freezer."

Ted knelt down on the other side of Jess. His face seemed to have aged ten years since last night. Just one more reason for Seth to feel guilty about his ill-advised decision to bring Jess here. He heaved a sigh, then glanced down at the object in his uncle's hand. And did a double take.

"I've seen that hat before!"

"So have I!" Willa exclaimed, stepping forward. "That's Lisa Harvey's!"

The onlookers began murmuring behind him. Seth looked around, catching sight of Lisa's pale face as she held up both hands and backed away from the mob.

"Wait a minute!" she gasped. "I had nothing to do with this!"

"It wasn't her."

All voices stilled as Jess's voice, hoarse and raw, remarked from her place on the floor.

"I saw her out the window just moments before I

was attacked. She couldn't have come back in so fast without me knowing it."

Seth wasn't convinced. If Lisa, or Bob for that matter, had someone working with them, it would have been easy enough for them to make the attack happen without getting their hands dirty.

"Why attack her here? There are so many people around." Seth tilted his head at his aunt. Her face was stiff with disapproval. At Jess or at the fact that someone could behave so poorly at her house, he wasn't sure. Seth had a theory about the attack, but it wasn't something he intended to discuss in front of a crowd. One of whom might be the person responsible.

One thing was sure. He didn't plan on giving the attacker another opportunity to harm Jess.

"Seth." Jess reached out a hand, slowly, her reflexes still sluggish, and touched his face. "You've been hurt."

He wanted to close his eyes and enjoy the feel of the hand on his face. For so many years, he'd pushed away women. Now this girl from his past was getting under his skin. Gently, he removed her hand from his face. It was too intimate. But he couldn't bring himself to let go of her hand completely. It might have been the selfishness he inherited from his arrogant father, but he craved the comfort she brought.

"I'll tell you about it when we're alone. Don't worry about it. I'm more concerned about the fact that someone in my uncle's house tried to kill you."

SIX

An hour later, once Jess had recovered enough to move, Seth and Jess retreated back to her room. Seth had warned Jess about the mess Bob had made of her things, but she still blanched when the door swung open. It looked a whole lot worse in the morning light than he had imagined. The fancy dress she had brought was crumpled in a heap on the floor. Those big hazel eyes puddled and blinked. Seth prepared himself for tears.

She surprised him, though. Her hands clenched into fists and her jaw tightened. "I thank You, Father, that Seth and I are alive."

What? Her room had been trashed and she was thankful? He tried to wrap his brain around that.

Turning his attention back to Jess, he saw that she had stiffened her resolve and was moving toward the pile of her belongings, which were still dumped on the bed where Bob had left them. Methodically, she sorted the items, her eyes fierce. With a glad cry, she located her batteries. Her hands shook so hard she dropped the tiny, round battery while trying to insert it into the hearing aid. Thankfully, it landed on the bed and didn't roll off.

"It works!" she sighed a minute later.

Seth dug out the other one. "Sorry, Jess. This one's toast. Fixing hearing aids wasn't taught in paramedic school."

To his astonishment, she gave a dry chuckle and shook her head. Why had he never noticed that dimple on her right cheek? It was adorable. The sudden urge to run his finger down her cheek shook him. He reminded himself that he was not here to romance her.

Pulling his mind back to the matter at hand, he tried to work out the best course of action. It was imperative that he keep Jess safe. That much was clear. Also clear was the fact that it wasn't going to be easy in this house.

An idea began to form in his mind. But would it work?

"We can't stay here."

Nice. Just blurt it out, Travis.

Her wide eyes spoke of her surprise. But she said nothing. He switched to sign, just in case there were ears at the door.

"I'm serious, Jess. We have to leave. I think our being here has scared whoever is after you past the point of caution. If that fall down the stairs had killed you—" she winced, but he kept going "—that would have looked like an accident. But it didn't, and you were able to tell someone you were pushed. Someone who believed you. And obviously, Uncle Ted believes you, and his opinion carries a lot of weight in the horse community. I don't know. But knocking you out and locking you in the freezer wasn't subtle at all, so apparently they're done making any attempts a secret. We're sitting ducks here."

"And how are we supposed to leave? And, even if we

do leave, where would we go? The power is still down and the creek's still flooded," she countered, following his lead and signing.

She had a point. The situation wasn't ideal, but he wasn't an Eagle Scout for nothing. He was always prepared.

"We're just going to have to rough it," he announced. Now she was looking worried. "I have my camping pack in the bed of my truck. It has my rock-climbing equipment, camping gear, and stuff like that. I will get it and we will leave quietly at the first opportunity."

"Rock climbing?" Her eyebrows disappeared under her bangs. Again, he fought the urge to brush the soft fringe aside. What was the matter with him?

"Yeah. Rock climbing. I'm an assistant scout master with the local troop. I teach the rock climbing and rappelling merit badges. Just did it last weekend, in fact. Which is why I have the pack in my truck."

Okay, so he was trying to impress her. Just a little.

Her brows lowered. Her teeth gnawed at her full lower lip. Determined to avoid her brand of distraction, he turned his gaze out the window. Still raining. Although, it seemed to have let up some. Maybe things would look up soon.

"Seth."

Her voice made him turn around. "Yeah?"

She reverted back to sign for her next words. "We're about five miles out from where Rebecca's parents live."

"Do you trust her family?" He was pretty sure he already knew the answer, but needed to make sure.

"Yeah. I'm sure her family would help us if we could just get to their house."

He considered it. "Where do they live?"

She told him. "Most of the houses on their street are owned by the Amish. And the lumber mill Levi works at is close by. We could probably get over there and use the business phone to call the police."

"Tomorrow—"

She interrupted him. "Tomorrow is Sunday. The family is very strict about no work on Sunday. We will have to wait to call until Monday."

Another day lost. Except at least they would be away from Jess's attacker.

"Better there than here. If we can sneak into the woods without being seen, we have a chance."

He waited for her slow nod.

"Let's do it."

Decision made, they made their way quietly downstairs, careful to keep away from the parts of the house where the rest of the guests were congregated. Ted had decreed that he wanted the others to stick together in the main part of the house. No one alone, just in case someone else were to become a target. Not that anyone believed for a second that anyone was in danger except for Jess.

Ted had told Seth privately that he wanted to keep an eye on the Harveys. And on Vic Horn, the cowboy who had accosted Jess in the hall and the one who was seen talking with Lisa Harvey just minutes before the attack. Ted had recognized him by Jess's description. Trouble was, no one seemed to able to find said cowboy. Vic Horn was nowhere to be found.

Which, in Seth's mind, put him at the top of the list of suspects. Just above the Harveys.

Muted voices drifted from the main part of the house. Even from a distance, it was clear the day's events had put a damper on everyone's spirits. Lifting his hand, he signed to Jess that the others were in the front room area. She nodded, hazel eyes shadowed, but made no reply. What was going through her mind?

Footsteps were headed toward them. He could hear the heels of cowboy boots on the wooden floor. Uncle Ted. He was the only one who dared wear shoes on Aunt Willa's pristine floors. He smirked, and glanced back at Jess. Then did a double take. She grabbed his hand, eyes wide.

"Someone's coming, I can feel the vibrations," she signed with her other hand, her movements jerky.

"It's okay," he reassured her, "it's Ted."

"Oh."

Her cheeks warmed and she dropped her eyes, obviously embarrassed by her reactions. When her eyes landed on their hands, still joined, her flush deepened and she tugged her hand away from his. Reluctantly, he let her go.

Ted rounded the corner, his face one dark thundercloud. The expression was so different from the normal jovial uncle he was used to, it gave Seth pause.

The warmth at his back increased. Jess had moved in closer, tucking herself neatly into his protection. Seth almost smiled. He liked the thought of her turning to him as her knight in shining armor. Except his armor was tarnished.

The thought wiped any smile off his face. He was no one's hero. He had learned long ago that he had too much in common with his father, no matter how hard he tried to be different. If he said he'd do something, it was as good as done. He never broke his word. Nor was he scared of hard work. But he'd hurt Jess. He'd let down his former fiancée when she'd needed him years before. When it came to women, he knew he couldn't be trusted.

Ted stomped to a halt in front of him.

Seth waited.

"Those people in there are driving me nuts," his uncle finally said.

This time, Seth cracked an amused grin. "Those people always drive me nuts. But what's getting to you?"

Ted gave him a glare for his trouble. "Well, Vic Horn still hasn't shown up. And the Harveys are apparently everyone's scapegoat for what happened. Not that they don't look the guiltiest, especially with Bob's antics. What was he looking for in her room, anyway?"

Seth shook his head. He wasn't in the mood to go over it right now. "Later."

Ted shrugged. "Fine. Anyway, Bob is trying to divert blame from his wife by insisting that your girl there locked herself in the freezer to make us feel sorry for her."

Jess gasped. "I did not!"

Holding up his hands and wagging his head, Ted shushed her. "Honey, I know you didn't. It's not physically possible to lock the door from the inside."

"I need to get her outta here," Seth declared, keeping his voice low. "Can I borrow your hip-waders? I need to get stuff from my truck and it's still surrounded by water."

"Yep."

Wearing the hip-high boots and suspenders, Seth stole from the house and splashed his way over to the truck. Twice he started to slip as his boots squished on the drenched grass beneath his feet. He couldn't afford

to walk down the meandering driveway…too out in the
open for anyone looking out the windows. Arriving at
the passenger side of the truck, he reached in behind the
seat for his backpack. In his mind, he debated whether
or not he should go through the pack, just to lighten the
load, getting rid of anything unnecessary. No time, he
decided. Mind made up, he hauled it out and strapped
it around himself. Done. He glanced up. And frowned.

Jess was standing outside of the house, her back
pressed against the bricks.

Why hadn't she stayed inside?

Every nerve was on high alert as she watched Seth
grabbing his pack. He was staying low, but she could
still see him over the window.

A gasp left her when he suddenly motioned for her
to hide, then ducked behind the truck himself.

Hide? Where could she go? And what was coming?

That's when she picked up the indistinct murmur of
voices. For her to be able to hear them with only one
hearing aid in place meant that they were closer than
was safe. She wasn't able to isolate individual voices,
but the group was heading her way.

Keeping her back against the wall, she pushed herself
into the bushes lined up parallel to the house, wincing
as branches scraped her face. She was small, but the
space between the shrubs and the building was practically nonexistent. She found herself literally between
branches. She had no idea how she'd escape without
being flayed or getting her hair pulled out.

If she escaped.

The voices came closer. She edged farther into her
hiding place. Three figures rounded the corner. Bob

and Lisa Harvey, and…Willa Taylor? Leaning in, she tried to catch part of their conversation. But between having just one aid, the loud roar of the rushing creek, the rain and the pounding of her own heart, she was only able to catch a random word here and there. And she couldn't lip read from this distance.

They seemed to be arguing. Willa's long face was pinched, her lips pursed. Lisa was stomping along beside her, mouth screwed up in an angry scowl. Both women appeared to be unhappy with whatever Bob was telling them. His loud voice boomed out, and Jess was able to hear part of what he said.

"…thief. Only way… Not going to jail for murder."

Jess shuddered. Had the trio tried to murder her? Were they responsible for the attacks and accidents?

Another thought hit her hard. Willa was Seth's aunt. What if he had lead her into an ambush deliberately? Sure, she had asked him to bring her to the party, but he hadn't protested that hard. Not really.

But he'd wanted her to go to the police. Yeah, but he'd picked his brother-in-law, who conveniently wasn't home.

And he had admitted his father used people to forward his own agenda. It was possible that Seth was like his father in that way.

No, it wasn't.

He could have let her die in the freezer, she argued with herself. Could have let her fall to her death down the stairs. But both times, he had saved her. And he had protected her all night. Back and forth, she went over the incidents in her mind. Her heart said to trust him, that he had changed since high school, and was now a man of his word. Her mind, though, urged caution. She couldn't allow herself to be blinded by her emotions.

Thinking of Seth, she worried that the trio walking past would see him and catch on to their plans to get away. Craning her neck, she peered toward the truck, only to become frustrated when the prickly branches blocked her view. She had no idea if he had been found or not. Nor, she realized, did she have any way of knowing when it was safe for her to rise from her hiding place.

Tentatively, she pulled her head back. Ouch! Her hair was caught, tangled up in the shrubbery in at least four places. Her fingers trembled and her eyes watered as she worked to free each strand. Twice, she gasped as thorns pricked her tender flesh. Her efforts finally paid off, and she was able to stand back. Her throat was dry as she poked her head up to get a cautious look around her.

No one was there.

Willa and the Harveys had disappeared.

But what about Seth? A breath she hadn't realized she was holding exploded from her as she watched his curly hair rise up from behind the truck so he could assess the area. His eyes were sharp as he glanced away. Almost remote. But they seemed to warm with relief when they landed on her.

Without a word, he motioned for her to meet him near the back of the house. She nodded to show her understanding, then painfully began to inch her way out of the bushes. Heart pounding, she forced herself to move past the large picture window, thankful that the curtains were still drawn. Although there was a tiny gap in the center where someone could see her if they had been looking that direction at just the right moment.

Shaking her head to forcibly stop that thought from gaining hold of her imagination, she continued on, step by terrifying step. She had never felt as vulnerable as she did now. Even in high school, she feared only bullies who would harass and humiliate her but had no interest in physically harming her. Now, she was afraid someone would leap out and kill her.

When she finally arrived to meet Seth, he still didn't say a word. Instead, he grabbed hold of her cold hand and started walking toward the woods behind his uncle's house.

Unable to resist, Jess looked back over her shoulder. The rain had stopped, and the house and grounds looked peaceful. The flooded creek was still swollen, angrily rushing and churning. The bridge…well, the bridge wasn't. Not anymore. It was buried under the water.

They had no choice.

Setting her jaw, she turned back and followed Seth. Whether or not he had an agenda, he was her only hope right now.

Not her only hope. She sent up a swift prayer. *Protect us, Lord. Keep us safe. And please let Seth be someone I can trust.*

It didn't take long before walking quietly through the mud and the muck grew old. Her boots frequently met resistance when she set her feet down in a particularly squishy spot, forcing her to slow down to jerk her foot loose.

Five miles. They had to move five miles to reach the Miller house, most of it through Amish country. If they were on the main road, there would even be a sign that announced to tourists Welcome to Amish Country.

Lots of hills. Lots of dirt roads. There would be businesses and traffic on the main street, but most of the traffic around the Millers would be buggies and the occasional truck. It would either be the best place to hide from a killer or the easiest place to be found.

She shuddered. Not a thought she wanted in her head at the moment, thank you very much. She'd had enough of being chased by a maniac to last her several lifetimes. Her mind filled with the memory of being shoved down the stairs.

How far had they gone? Was it safe enough to talk? She had to say something or she'd go out of her mind from her own imagination.

"Seth!"

Seth whirled, his eyes jerking back and forth. Uh-oh. He thought there was trouble. She flinched. She hadn't meant to say his name that loud.

"Sorry. Just wondered if we could talk now? I'm going crazy with my own thoughts."

After a moment of hesitation, he nodded slowly, but his expression was wary. "We can talk," he said, signing as he spoke. It was a good thing—he was talking so softly she could barely make out what he was saying. "What do you want to discuss?"

Now was the time to lay her cards out on the table. See his reaction when his aunt's name was brought up. Caution kept her tongue still even as every instinct told her he wasn't involved in anything.

When she didn't say anything, he shrugged and started to move again. She had no choice but to follow. Guess they weren't going to talk, after all. Swallowing a disappointed sigh, she trudged along, irritation brewing.

A moment later, he slowed down so they could walk side by side.

"Tell me about Cody," he said, breaking the silence and jarring her composure with the quick intrusion into her personal life. "But only if you want to?"

Huh? Oh, she hadn't replied. Did she want to tell him about Cody? Yes, she was shocked to say she did.

"Sorry. Didn't mean to shut down on you there. You startled me that's all." What to say? "Cody was a really good guy. And a great brother. He was the only one in my family who really got me, you know?" She took his quick half smile as acknowledgment and plunged ahead. "When we were growing up, my parents were so busy working, often it was just the two of us. He didn't care that I needed him to face me when he talked. Or that I sometimes needed him to sign. His friends told him I was faking to get attention, using my deafness like a game."

"I have noticed that sometimes you seem to do better at reading lips than others."

She nodded. There hadn't been any censure in his expression, she was relieved to note. Only acceptance. "Yeah. English is a tricky thing. So many words look the same. And then some voices I can hear better than others. Mostly male voices."

"I noticed that."

She tossed him a smirk. "And then there are some people who cover their mouths with their hands while they talk. Or barely move their mouths…"

"Or have beards," he interrupted with an air of revelation. "Ernie once said if he were president he would ban full beards and mustaches."

She choked back a laugh, not wanting to be too loud. "Yeah, beards can be really bad."

Sobering, she let her mind drift over memories of

growing up with Cody. "What I really loved about Cody was his gentleness. He was truly hurt by cruelty toward horses. The foundation was his passion. He was driven to protect and rescue the horses. There's no way he would have stolen money. Or done anything to injure the horses. And he was very devout. I refuse to believe he would or could go against God that way."

Seth shuffled a bit, head down.

"Sorry, I didn't mean to make you uncomfortable."

A hint of a smile flickered on his face and was gone.

"No. That's okay. Growing up in my house, I learned skepticism at a young age."

What did you say to that? Except, "You want to talk about it?"

He shook his head. Then seemed to change his mind. "My mom was sick for as long as I could remember. I learned early on that my dad wasn't faithful to her. They went to church every week, and still he cheated on her. Joe Travis, such a great family man."

Bitterness twisted his mouth. "It really hit home one day when I was in high school. I think it was just after you left. I came home and my mom was unconscious on the floor. I called 911. And I tried to call my dad but his office staff had no idea where he was. The paramedics showed up just as my mom started having a seizure. I know they saved her life. My dad arrived after she was already at the hospital. He looked worried, said all the right things, but when I got close to him, I saw that he had the proverbial lipstick on his collar. I used to think that was such a cliché. Until I saw it on my old man."

He stalked away a few feet, leaned with one hand against a tree. Her heart broke for him. She went to him and placed a hand on his shoulder. Her hand trembled. So did his shoulder.

He moved away, and her hand dropped back to her side. When he turned back to her, his face had been wiped clean of all emotion.

Beckoning with his head, he indicated that they should continue moving.

Desperate for a positive direction to take the conversation, she focused on the rest of what he'd said—the way the paramedics had saved his mother.

"Is that why you became a paramedic?" she asked.

"Yes. And it's also why I haven't set foot in a church, outside of a few weddings and funerals here and there, since high school. I figure God kinda turned His back on me. So I just returned the favor."

SEVEN

They wound their way through the woods until Jess no longer had any sense of which direction they were traveling in. The rain-scented mist filled her nostrils. Her boots sank into the wet earth with each step. Gradually, her socks became wet. She must have a crack somewhere in her supposedly waterproof boots. Great. Just what she needed.

Still, she said nothing. Just followed where Seth lead. Every now and then, he glanced down at the compass he had pulled from his pack. But he never slowed, never appeared unsure of where they were going.

She had to admit, she was pretty impressed with him so far. He was showing a side of himself she never would have imagined. It was no longer a stretch to picture him teaching survival skills to a group of eager boys.

He slowed, and turned to face her. It never failed to amaze her how aware of her need to see his face he was. It wasn't that he rarely forgot. He *never* forgot. Ever.

"How are you doing?"

"Fine." She didn't want to admit her feet were getting wet and sore. What good would it do? He raised his brows, tilting his head to give her a searching glance. Obviously, he wasn't convinced.

"Are you sure?" he asked. "We've probably only gone about a mile and a half. I can still hear the creek, so we're going in the right direction."

That surprised her. "The creek?"

He nodded. "Yeah, we have to follow it for about three miles, then head west for the last two."

"Okay." Restraining the sigh that wanted to break free, she gave him what she hoped was a willing smile.

And received a concerned look from his brown eyes in return.

She really needed to work on her acting skills.

"Look, Jess, I wish we could rest, but my gut says we need to keep going. Sooner or later someone will notice we are gone. And I want to be far away when that happens."

"I'm not complaining. Let's keep going."

He sighed, straightened his pack, and they started off again.

Five minutes later, they spotted the creek. It looked less frightening, now that they were above it. She could still see that it was higher than normal, but from this height, it was hard to determine how much higher.

Jess opened her mouth to comment. The comment was never made, however, as Seth whirled and threw a sharp glance behind them.

"I hear voices," he signed.

She felt the blood draining from her face. There was nothing to hold anyone back from openly attacking her out here. And it was quite possible if they were killed, no one would ever find the bodies.

Seth grabbed hold of her hand and pulled her off

the path. They moved at an angle, forward and closer to the creek, taking care to stay in the grass. *No tracks,* she thought.

"There's an old path a little below us," he signed. "If we're quiet, we can use it, and hopefully no one will even know we're there."

Trepidation filled her as they walked closer to the edge of the shallow cliff. Looking down, she could clearly see a narrow path...about fifty feet below. Wildly, she whipped her gaze in Seth's direction. He was kidding, right?

Nope. He was digging through his pack, bringing out ropes and a harness.

Her stomach lurched, but she swallowed hard to force it under control. If she got sick right here, that would leave a real clue as to where they were.

In spite of her trepidation, there was no way she could argue with Seth's plan. They needed to leave this area. Every second they were closer to being found.

With sure and swift hands, Seth harnessed her and attached the rope.

"I'm going to lower you down. When you get to the path, move to the side, and keep your back against the cliff until I join you."

She nodded, then allowed him to start lowering her. He had wrapped the rope around a tree, using it as a sort of pulley. His biceps bulged as he held the rope with both hands, using a foot against the tree to assist him in controlling the speed of her descent. She would have appreciated the sight a whole lot more if it weren't for the terror racing through her system.

Her mind blank with panic, all she could think was, *Please, Lord. Please, Lord.* All the way down, she repeated her litany until her feet touched the path. The relief was so great, her knees started to buckle. Stiffening her legs, she remembered Seth's directions and backed up against the wall over to the side, waiting for Seth. It seemed to take forever. What if he was having a problem? The sudden thump of his pack landing beside her made her start.

She looked up, and thought her heart had stopped.

Seth was on his way down, but he was climbing, rock by rock. Once he missed the rock with his foot, and in her mind, she could she him tumbling backward and over the edge to the creek below. Shoving her knuckles in her mouth to stifle any cries that might distract him, she watched, spellbound, as he made his way to her.

When he was a couple of feet above the path, he allowed himself to drop the rest of the way. Jess didn't stop to think. She pushed herself away from the cliff and threw both arms around his waist, burying her head in his neck. She couldn't stop shaking.

For about two seconds, Seth was still. Then his arms gently closed around her, and his hands rubbed her back. She felt his lips touch her hair.

Calmer, she backed out of his arms, slightly ashamed of her outburst. He didn't seem bothered by it. His kind eyes searched her face. Then, apparently satisfied, he backed away, letting his own arms drop. With a rapidity that could only come from hours of practice, he had his gear repacked and his pack back on his shoulders.

"It's okay," he signed. "Let's move along this path." He bent his knees and brought his face level with hers. Trying to see directly into her eyes, she realized. Feeling self-conscious, she ducked her head. After a second, she glanced up under her lashes at him to find he was still focused on her face, a concerned twist to his mouth.

"I'm fine," she signed.

She tried to still her trembling as he ran his eyes over her again. She was beginning to recognize that gaze as his paramedic one. It was focused and detached. But she thought she detected warmth in it.

His sudden grin distracted her. Cocky. Yeah, she remembered that grin. She felt herself grinning back without knowing why. His smile had always had that effect.

"It's a good thing I didn't lighten my pack." He signed. "I debated on it, and decided not to."

She held in her snort. Barely.

"It wasn't just chance, you know. It was the inspiration of the Holy Spirit. God knew we would need that stuff. He's always watching over us, trying to guide us. But He won't force His will on us. The choice is ours."

The discomfort that covered his face made her roll her eyes. Somehow she'd get through to him.

Or maybe not. *Lord, use me to bring Seth back to You. And if not me, then bring him in contact with someone who will.*

God could handle it from here. They had wasted enough time. She dropped the subject.

"Let's just keep moving."

The tension melted from his expression. He nodded and readjusted his pack. Then with a confidence she could only envy, he moved down the narrow path. Swallowing, she made the mistake of glancing down at the creek. Whoa. For a moment, she battled nausea. Sucking in deep breaths of cool air helped. There was something soothing about the smell of the forest.

"We are in Your hands, Lord. I trust You."

It helped to keep one hand on the wall of dirt and rock beside her as she walked. It also made her feel safer when she noticed that Seth kept checking on her. Despite her earlier fears about him, she now felt sure that he would do everything he could to keep her safe.

She had no concept of how long they traveled on that narrow path. The wind had kicked up, stinging her cheeks and making her eyes water as she trudged along. She had to frequently blink to clear her blurred vision.

What really made her anxious was that she had no idea what was happening up above. Her neck tingled with the feeling that there were eyes watching her. Her one good hearing aid was picking up the sound of the creek and amplifying it to the point that she was incapable of hearing anything else. Even if there were voices directly overhead, she would never hear them. Just one more way she was completely dependent on Seth.

No sooner had the thought popped into her mind than he abruptly stopped walking and half whirled toward her, eyes shooting her a desperate warning. Jess stopped dead in her tracks. What was she supposed to do?

Seth took care of that for her. Hurrying back to where she stood, he grabbed on to her and pulled her back with him up against the rocks. They stood silently together, hidden by a small overhang. If she moved forward three inches, she would be out of its protection. Her body started to tremble as she realized what was happening.

Someone was above them. She still couldn't hear anyone, but she saw the rocks and debris that tumbled down past them from someone standing on the edge over their heads. Jess buried her face against Seth and squeezed her eyes shut. Beneath her cheek she felt the solid thud of his heart.

She focused on keeping her breathing calm. All she could do was stand still until Seth gave her a sign that it was clear.

They were trapped.

There were at least two people above him. Seth could hear the feet shuffling as one walked north and the other south. Then they moved together again. His body tensed as he heard the footsteps coming closer to the edge. Instinct had him holding Jess tighter, presser their bodies closer to the rocks. She was trembling, and the hand gripping his was like ice.

Probably a mixture of cold and fear. When they escaped from this situation, he'd have to see what he could do about making her warmer.

For a second, he allowed himself to cast his eyes down at her face. Then he looked longer. What he had expected to see was fear and anxiety. Maybe some tears. Instead, her forehead was pressed against his shoulder, but her face was calm. Her lips were moving soundlessly.

She was praying. He should have figured.

The thought bothered him, but not as much as it would have a week ago. He remembered praying briefly while searching for her earlier that morning. Looking back, he realized that brief prayer had refocused him, given him a small measure of peace. Peace that he'd been too busy working to save her life to analyze. Yet now, here in the forest, he realized that he had sensed something.

Maybe God hadn't completely abandoned him.

Tentatively, he said a quick prayer for help. Not that

he was sure how much good it would do, but it wouldn't hurt. Surely, they were sitting ducks until the people on the ledge moved.

Or found them.

He drew Jess closer, rubbing his chin against her soft hair. He had failed too many people in the past. Jess. His mom. Melanie. He had let his fear of becoming like his father cripple him emotionally. Now was his chance to set things to right. If that meant putting himself at risk to protect the woman in his arms, so be it. If need be, he was certain he could distract those after her so she could run to safety.

He frowned, feeling uneasy. That would only work if she would run. He had already learned that she had a core of loyalty. Chances of her leaving him to deal with the bad guys weren't good.

"They ain't here!" a voice boomed out above, rich with belligerence. The voice was so loud, it echoed several times. It was a voice he was unfamiliar with.

Jess jerked her head up, eyes wide. So she had heard the man, too.

The man's partner must have answered, even though he couldn't hear it, because the man continued speaking.

"Disguise my voice? What for? I tell you, there ain't no one here but us and the squirrels.

"You know what? I think you're just paranoid. No one's going to connect her getting stuck in a freezer to me. I didn't leave that many footprints. Besides, all those other idiots trampled on my footprints."

Silence. He was probably listening to whatever the other person was saying.

"And I'm sick an' tired of you giving me orders!"

Now the man sounded angry. There was a definite sneer in his voice. "I'm not getting paid enough to take that from you. It ain't my fault she didn't die. If you had done your part—"

The other person must have said or done something to cut him off because he was silent for a moment before releasing an ugly laugh. Seth had never heard a laugh so cold and vicious. What kind of monsters were they dealing with?

"I'll tell you what," his voice came again, silky and dangerous. "Let's just renegotiate our deal. I think my price has just increased. Doubled. The kind of things you want done aren't easy. Or cheap. And don't think I'm messing around, here, either. It would be no skin off my back to let you take the rap for everything."

A laugh—but not the same one from before. Seth's head shot up, shock making his mouth drop open. Was that a woman's laugh? It was so muffled, it was hard to tell. He looked at Jess. She didn't look like she had heard it. Either it was too soft, or too high pitched for her to catch it.

Who did it sound like? It was so brief, how could he say for sure?

Was it Aunt Willa? No, he couldn't believe that. It would devastate Ted. And his aunt wasn't that cruel, was she? But he remembered the coldness of her eyes as she had looked at Jess when they had first arrived. His stomach tightened.

What about Lisa Harvey? Her hat had been found in the freezer. Maybe this guy had left it there as some sort of insurance.

Even in the cold, he was starting to sweat.

"Wait! What are you doing?" the man said, sudden

panic in his voice. "Put that down! There's no reason we can't talk about this calm—"

A shot rang out. The woods filled with clatter as dozens of startled birds squawked and flew from their branches.

Jess flinched back against the rock, gasping. Seth covered her mouth with his hand, his heart beating wildly in his chest.

Seth heard a shuffling noise above. Like something large being pushed...or dragged...

Jess looked up, her eyes widening. Noting the color draining from her face, Seth followed her gaze...just in time to see a body start to tip over the edge. Pressing them both against the rocks, he covered Jess with his body as much as he could to protect her. The man's hand brushed against his boot as he tumbled past them and disappeared into the angry waters below. Seth could see his lifeless face pop out of the water once before it was pulled under again.

Vic Horn.

So now they knew who had locked Jess up in the freezer. But on whose orders?

Hunched down, they waited for Vic's partner to finish searching. From the sound of things, the shooter was cleaning up. Possibly getting rid of evidence. A flurry of leaves and debris fluttered past them. Maybe Vic's blood had spilled on the leaves. He wished he could be certain it was a woman who was responsible—it would cut the list of suspects in half. If only he could hear the shooter's voice.

And how was he supposed to do that? Yell up and say, "Hey, you who just shot this guy and tossed him over the edge…are you male or female?" He almost snorted at the thought.

Then his glance fell on the creek where mere seconds before Vic Horn's lifeless body had fallen.

He shuddered. He was trained to save lives. Sure, he'd had his share of patients die. But not before he had done his best to save them. The casual way Vic's partner had shot him and tossed him away like so much garbage was not something he could easily understand. Even more incredible was the fact that it was likely someone he knew who had done it. Incomprehensible.

But what he did understand was that the person mere feet above them would eliminate him and Jess in the same manner without blinking an eye.

Not if he could help it.

He wasn't a cop or former soldier like his brother-in-law, but he did know how to survive.

Maybe half an hour went by before he felt they could safely move. It had been twenty minutes since any noise had drifted down to them.

Moving slowly, he pushed himself away from the rocks and away from Jess. No one shot him. Letting out a breath, he ran an assessing glance over Jess. She looked tired. And she was shivering. But otherwise seemed to be holding up. Ignoring her protests, he shrugged out of his jacket. He was warm enough in his layers of clothing. And her jacket wasn't doing the job.

"You need to stay warm," he signed. "We still have at least an hour or two ahead of us."

Seth bit back a smile at the disgruntled frown she sent him before she reluctantly agreed and put his coat on. A surge of affection welled up inside him. She was adorable in the oversize coat. Her hazel eyes and ponytail made her look almost fragile. But he knew she had strength. And determination.

He was relying on that determination now.

EIGHT

Jess tugged Seth's collar up closer to her nose and inhaled. She had noticed how good he smelled before. Now she was overwhelmed by the scent.

Of course, being warm was rather nice, too. For a while, she had wondered if she would ever feel warm again. Now, everything was toasty, except her feet. And she knew they wouldn't be warm until she could get out of these old boots. Which meant not until they reached the Millers' house.

She wished she could talk to Seth. It would take her mind off the sight of Vic Horn slamming into the current and being carried away. A shiver worked its way up her spine. She rubbed the spot on her neck that had burned before she'd blacked out and woken up in the freezer. It had to have been a needle of some kind. Knowing that he had so callously drugged her and dragged her into the freezer to die was horrible. Knowing someone else was also in on it was unspeakable.

According to Seth, who had given her a quick recap of what he'd heard before they'd started walking again, the other voice might have been female. Unless that was a disguise.

Seth had a disturbed look around his eyes, and his mouth was tight as he looked over his shoulder at her. It made her ache inside. It didn't take much to understand he was worried that his aunt might be involved in all this. She wished she could take that pain away from him, but knew it was impossible.

Still, the need to offer him some sort of comfort wouldn't let her go. Half an hour later, they left the narrow path beside the creek and headed west toward the Millers' house. They were forced to slog through the mud and leaves between the trees, but there was one benefit. There was room to move side by side.

Without giving herself a chance to talk herself out of it, Jess quickened her step and moved up beside Seth. He gave her a startled glance when she took his hand. Embarrassed, and afraid he might take offense, she started to move away. But found he wouldn't release her hand. Instead, he gripped it, squeezing slightly while giving her a sad smile. Well, not really a smile. Just the corners of his lips curling up. But he seemed to understand her intent.

"Thanks," he mouthed.

She nodded.

The sky was growing dark when they left the woods and found themselves on a dirt road. The houses were spaced far apart, but they had definitely reached the Amish community. The first house they passed was a large farmhouse with a woman in a plain blue dress and a white prayer *kapp* sweeping the front porch. She gave them a smile and bobbed her head as they passed. Two little girls splashed through the puddles in the front yard.

"How far is it?" Seth asked, still signing while he talked.

"Near the end of this road," she replied. She didn't bother to sign. He could understand her just fine. She pointed to her left. "We're about a mile from the middle of town, that way. There isn't a lot of car traffic on this road. Although if we were to go to the end of this road, there's another paved road. It's a main road, so it's pretty busy."

After what seemed like forever, they arrived at the Miller house. No one was outside, and Jess started to feel panicky. What if no one was home? She knew they had family in Ohio. Sometimes the family traveled there to visit. What if...?

The door opened as they walked up to the wide, wrap-around porch. They came face to face with Levi, whose eyes were wide and troubled.

"Jess? What are you doing here? Rebecca is not here."

She had to work to understand him. Between his accent and his habit of barely moving his lips while he talked, he had always been a challenge to understand. Thankfully, he was the best signer in the Miller family, so she could always ask him to sign if necessary. Although she would save that for a last resort. She knew that Levi wasn't comfortable switching to sign.

"I know, Levi. Do you remember Seth, the paramedic?" Impatience made her talk quicker than usual. Any moment she expected someone to burst from the woods brandishing a gun.

"*Jah*. I remember. It is *gut* to see you again."

Yeah, it might have been good, but he still looked troubled.

"Levi, I'm sorry to intrude, but can we come in? We're in serious trouble."

Silently, the serious young man swung his kind eyes between them. Finally, he nodded.

"*Jah*. You are always welcome, Jess. Mam and Dat will be pleased to see you."

Swinging the door wide, he motioned for them to enter the house.

Jess needed no further invitation. She entered the house, being careful to remove her muddy boots just inside the door. Seth did the same. She hurried into the large, warm kitchen area, aware of Seth at her heels. Rebecca's mother, Martha, turned from where she stood cooking at the large stove. Jess sniffed in appreciation, her stomach rumbling as the smell of homemade stew hit her nostrils.

"Jessica!" Martha said in her strongly accented English. "We did not expect you to visit. Is the flooding gone?"

Martha's keen blue eyes swept over Jess and Seth. Jess flushed, realizing the picture they made. A quick glance at Seth showed that he was dirty and looked ready to collapse. It wasn't hard to imagine that she probably looked about the same, maybe even a little worse after trekking through the woods and going over a cliff. And she was still wearing Seth's jacket, which hung on her smaller frame.

She cleared her throat, but Seth beat her at answering.

"No ma'am. I'm Jess's friend Seth. We were stranded on this side of the creek when it flooded, and haven't been able to get home yet."

Alarm filled Martha's round face. "Have you been out in this weather all this time?"

"No, we were at my uncle's house when it started."

Jess could see the confusion cross Martha's face. She had a fairly good idea of what the woman was thinking. Why would they leave the comfort of his relatives' house and travel here? A sudden dread struck her. What if the Millers felt they were too high risk to let them stay? She had never known them to turn anyone away, but what if her situation was just too much for them to take on?

Her nerves and the cold caught up with her all at once. Her body began to tremble with a vengeance. Even tugging Seth's jacket around her did nothing to lessen the chill sweeping over her slender frame. The chattering of her teeth caused her jaw to ache.

An arm around her shoulder startled her. Seth. Looking up at him, she noted vaguely that he looked blurry.

"She's half frozen. And ready to collapse," she heard him say close to her good ear.

Martha swiftly crossed the room to her, and hustled her to a chair near the wood burning stove. She gave Levi a firm command. Jess couldn't understand it, but she recognized the sounds of Pennsylvania Dutch. Levi answered in the same language, then stoked up the fire inside.

Soon, she found herself seated, her soggy socks replaced with a clean pair of thick, warm ones. It took another fifteen minutes for her to feel truly warm. When Martha brought her a bowl of hearty stew and a thick slab of homemade bread, she accepted gratefully, thanking her hostess with feeling.

Between the food and the warmth of the fire, she began to nod off. Only through sheer will did she manage to remain awake. She focused her attention on where Seth was seated with Martha and Levi. It took some effort, but she managed to catch most of the conversation flowing between them as Seth explained their situation.

Martha and Levi seemed genuinely shocked and concerned about the predicament they found themselves in. Although not, she was glad to note, in any apparent hurry to shoo them out the door. If anything, Martha's face started to resemble that of a mother bear as she heard about someone literally gunning for her daughter's oldest friend.

Warmth tugged at Jess's heart. It had been so long since she had felt so protected. The feeling was followed by an ache at the realization that such moments were going to be rare for her, and not permanent. After all, she had no family anymore, and her prospects were low.

But she wasn't going to sit here and have a pity party. Straightening in her chair, she narrowed her gaze on Seth's solemn face. The sudden longing in her soul took her by surprise. She remembered her doubts about him earlier. Was that really only several hours ago? Now, looking at his honest face, she couldn't believe she had wondered if she could trust him. He had put himself in harm's way for her more than once, and never once had he hesitated. He had more than proven himself worthy of her trust.

Shame grew in her as she realized that in doubting him, she was also, to some extent, doubting God. For she could clearly see God's hand in giving her the perfect protector. Who else would have known how to ensure they'd survive? Or how to save her when she was injured? Even his ability to sign proved that he was the perfect person to help her.

No more doubting, she decided. *From now on, Lord, I will trust You and Your providence without fail.*

Which didn't mean she would be so foolish as to allow herself to make the huge mistake of falling for him. It would be so easy, she mused as she watched him shove his thick curls back from his forehead. She knew how devastating his charm could be. But even though she believed she could trust him, she also was aware of his determination to avoid any sort of emotional commitment. No, friendship was all she could ever share with him. She had to be satisfied with that.

But she wasn't satisfied. Her heart had already started to latch on to him.

Well, no more. She would just have to stay on her guard around him.

That resolution firm in her mind, she returned to the conversation in front of her, battling to keep her eyes open. At last, she gave in and let her weary eyelids drift shut, secure in the knowledge that she was safe.

At least for the moment.

Jess was snoring. Soft little purring sounds that made him think of a kitten.

Seth ducked his head, hiding his grin behind the mug of black coffee Martha had just set before him. His grin faded as he continued to watch her. She was exhausted and scuffed up. There were several scratches on her face and neck.

All at once, impatience swamped him. He wanted action. The need to move, to be doing something, to fix things, crawled over his skin.

Only when Levi gave him a pointed look did he realize his leg was furiously bouncing up and down, his heel making a staccato tapping sound on the hardwood floor. Abashed, he forced his leg to still.

"Sorry," he muttered.

Levi nodded, his eyes understanding. "You want to be active, *jah*?"

Seth blew out a breath and ran his hands over his face. "Yeah. I can't be easy until I know that whoever wants to hurt Jess is out of the way."

Martha stood and began to clear the table. "You must leave it in Gott's hands."

Sure. Easier said than done.

"There is nothing to be done this evening," Levi said. "Tomorrow, we can think more about it."

"Levi," Martha reproved her son. "Tomorrow is the Lord's day."

"*Jah*, I know, Mam. We will talk, not work. That will wait for Monday."

"Don't you have some kind of community phone?" He took a long slurp of coffee. Caffeine might not be healthy, but maybe it would jolt his system enough to keep him alert.

"*Jah*. We have one. It is not working now. It was hit by a tractor."

Seth winced. The small wooden phone booths used to house a single emergency phone would not be able to withstand the force of a large tractor crashing into it.

I now know what would make someone want to bang their head against a wall, Seth mused, twisting his mouth. Still, maybe a day of quiet would be a good thing. Jess obviously needed the rest. And the water level wouldn't be down enough for them to cross the creek and return to LaMar Pond until Monday, at the earliest. Although, he suspected the electricity would be back by tomorrow. It might even be back now, but not where he was at.

A new thought occurred to him. Was their sudden appearance throwing a wrench in the family's plans? Funny, he hadn't thought of it before, but now he shifted in his seat. He wasn't religious. Hadn't been inside a church since Maggie and Dan married. And even though he had prayed a couple of times in the past day or so, faith was still a bit of an alien concept to him. But for the Miller family, he suspected it was a way of life. And now he and Jess had disrupted this family's life without warning just before the Sabbath day.

"Um, I never thought... I mean, Jess and I, we don't want to get in the way of your plans. So, um, if you need to, you know, go to church or something tomorrow?" He let the unfinished question hang there, feeling his ears grow warm as both Levi and his mother smiled at him.

"We attend church every two weeks, and this is our at home week." Levi reassured him. "After you and Jessica rest tonight, I will help you plan your next move. Tomorrow."

And with that, he had to be satisfied.

If they could get to a phone, he could call Dan and bring him up to date on the facts. He knew his brother-in-law. Dan would take the situation seriously. Especially now that a body was involved. He and the rest of the police would want to drag the creek and search for Horn's body so they could process it for evidence, like the ballistics from the bullet that killed him.

The sawmill Levi worked at wasn't that far from here. Three miles? Four? If Levi would agree to bring them there to use the phone, a whole lot of problems could be solved. He mentioned his line of thought to Levi.

"Would the bullet help them find the person who killed the man who went over the cliff?"

Seth smiled. It was kind of refreshing to talk with someone who wasn't hooked on crime shows. He had gotten used to family members of patients questioning his decisions based on things they had seen on TV. Like that didn't get old fast.

"I can't be sure. I'm not a cop, but I think that sometimes bullets can be traced to a specific type of gun. Maybe even a single gun, if it's registered." He rolled his eyes at that.

"You don't think this will happen?"

A wry chuckle slipped out. "I find it highly unlikely that anyone would shoot someone with a gun registered in their own name. Unless it was an accident. And I doubt very much that this shooting was an accident. It's more likely that whoever shot Horn intended to kill him all along. Horn threatened her, but I don't think that made a difference."

"Her?" Levi's eyes sharpened. Martha gasped as she walked into the room and heard the last comment.

Seth colored. What a time to forget himself. That was not information he had planned on sharing. The Millers would be safer the less they knew.

"I can't be sure. But I thought I heard a laugh. It might have been a woman's. Or it might have just sounded that way because I was so far away."

"What was the name of the man who was killed?" Levi took a gulp of hot coffee, nodding his thanks to his mother, who continued to unobtrusively fuss over the men and straighten up the large, cozy room. Sitting so near the warmth of the fire as the scents of coffee and pine mingled in the air was making him feel a little drowsy himself. It was no wonder Jess had fallen asleep.

What had Levi asked? Oh, yeah. The name.

"Vic Horn. I assume that's short for Victor. I had never seen him before this weekend, and I thought I was pretty well acquainted with the horse crowd."

Levi rubbed his chin between his thumb and his forefinger, deep furrows creasing his forehead. "I have heard that name before."

Seth sat up, the sleepy fog that had started to envelop him disappearing.

"You have? Where?" In his excitement, he unintentionally raised his voice. Both Levi and Martha looked at him, startled. Flushing, he realized he had come half up out of his chair, his hands clenched on the wooden arms. "Sorry," he muttered, lowering himself back down into his seat.

Martha returned to her chores. Levi flashed an unexpected half smile at him. It transformed his solemn face, making him look youthful.

"I understand. You are anxious to find the person who would hurt Jessica. I do not remember where I have heard the name. I will try to remember so I can help you."

Disappointed, Seth nodded. How he wished he could do more.

Right now, though, he was too tired to do anything.

Martha had anticipated his needs. A bed in the small guest room had been made up with fresh sheets.

"Jessica can sleep in Rebecca's old room," the motherly woman announced.

Gently, Seth shook Jess's shoulder. She jerked awake, eyes wide with fear.

"Easy, Jess," he signed to her. "You'll be more comfortable in a bed. Mrs. Miller said you can sleep in Rebecca's room."

She reminded him of a little girl as she yawned and used her knuckles to rub the sleep out of her eyes.

"Where will you be?" She caught her lower lip in her teeth. Seth had seen that expression so often, yet now, seeing her tug at her lip made him wonder what it would be like to lean down and kiss her...

Whoa, boy! This is no time to be thinking of romance. And you are certainly not the man to be considering any long-term relationship. The old argument felt false now. He wished he could make a different choice. The decision to remain single and unattached had seemed so logical, but now it seemed like a cold future.

"I'll be down here, Jess. Don't worry. I will still be here in the morning."

He gave her what he hoped was an encouraging smile. Her smile back at him was somewhat confused, so he probably hadn't completely succeeded. But she let Martha lead her up the stairs without comment. He was strangely heartened when she looked back over her shoulder at him before she entered the room.

Then guilt struck. If she was starting to develop feelings for him, it would not end well for her. The last thing he wanted was to hurt her, again. Deep down, where he kept his feelings locked up, a round ball of fear festered. That fear that said he could never make any woman truly, lastingly happy. That he would never be worthy of a woman's love.

Jess's words in the woods wove through his brain, making his heart ache with longing for what he had always believed was out of reach. Could she be right? Was God watching over them, prompting them softly like a father? Was God just waiting for him to make the next move?

A wave of exhaustion crashed over him, and he felt himself swaying where he stood. Well, he was of no use to anyone like this.

A hand on his shoulder jerked him alert.

"Come," Levi said, "I will show you where you will sleep." Levi led him down a hall to a small bedroom near the back of the house. The room was big enough for a bed and a dresser, and not much else. Fine with him. Looking closer, gratitude seized him. A pair of plain blue pajamas had been set on the bed. He hadn't expected more than a place to rest for the night. Overwhelmed by the hospitality shown to him by these strangers, he thanked Levi in a choked voice.

Wishing Levi a good night, he entered the room and prepared for bed. Changed and comfortable, he took a closer look at his clothes, shaking his head. It was a wonder these people let him into their house! They were covered in mud, and he counted no less than five rips in his shirt. Probably from rock climbing without protective gear. Well, he couldn't regret that. Leaving a rope tied around a tree while he climbed down would have been like leaving a neon sign pointing directly to where he and Jess had been hiding. No. He would gladly accept a ripped up shirt if it meant that Jess was safe.

As tired as he was, he should have fallen asleep immediately. Instead, he tossed and turned, the events of the past couple days rumbling around in his head, like equations that he needed to solve. But he didn't have all the variables. Piece by piece, his mind sorted through the facts. Finally, he fell into a troubled sleep, dreaming of people falling off cliffs, bullet holes in their chests.

He was jerked from his restless slumber several hours later, heart pounding. Faint light was streaming in through the window. It had to be closing in on five in the morning.

Several dogs barked and growled ferociously right outside his window. A moment later, he heard something crashing. Running to the window, he was in time to see a shadowy figure limp away and disappear behind the barn. The dogs lurched forward on their chains, enraged, before they were jerked back by their collars. It couldn't be a coincidence that an intruder would come to the house mere hours after they had arrived. And that meant just one thing.

They had been found.

NINE

Seth rushed from his room, intent on stopping whoever was outside.

Levi beat him to the back door. Without wasting time, the Amish man handed Seth a lantern and headed outside. Even though the sun was coming up, it was still dark in the woods and in the barn. Soon they were joined by an older man. Mr. Miller, Seth assumed. It was hard to make out the man's features in the morning light. But what he could make out was the shape of a shotgun grasped in the older man's large hands.

Seth was shocked. He thought the Amish didn't believe in violence. He said as much to Levi.

"We will not shoot at a person, it is true," Levi explained in his slow, deep voice. "We have had trouble with foxes getting to our chickens."

Mr. Miller nodded. "I am certain that is what has upset the dogs."

The three men carefully circled the house.

"I don't know. I have a bad feeling that whoever is after Jess might have found us." Seth's eyes scanned the horizon. Shadows danced near the woods, playing tricks on his imagination.

Mr. Miller clucked his tongue. Seth knew disapproval when he heard it. "You must trust *Gott*. He will protect us."

Doubtful. Seth bit back a stinging retort, partially because he didn't want to be disrespectful toward the man who was allowing Seth and Jess to stay in his home. But also because, in spite of himself, a small sliver of doubt had managed to wedge itself into his soul. He could no longer ignore the questions that had started to plague him about faith. Questions, he realized, that he had locked deep inside for years, but which had never really gone away. Somewhere in his heart, he had always wanted to believe.

"I thought I saw someone limping away through there." Seth pointed in the direction of the barn. Levi inclined his head. Seth understood. Lead the way. A sigh of relief burst from him. They might not believe in violence, but they would stand by his side as he tracked whatever he had seen from inside the house. He set out at a quick walk, almost a jog, carefully scanning the area around them as he moved. He was aware of Levi and Mr. Miller silently jogging at his elbows.

Half an hour later, the men returned to the house, no closer to figuring out who or what the dogs had seen.

Mr. Miller didn't seem concerned. He mumbled something about trespassers as he shrugged out of his jacket. Then he replaced his gun and returned to his room.

Seth stared after him, unsure what to do. "Levi, what if the trespasser was whoever's after Jess? I can't shake the feeling that we've been found."

"How?" Levi said in his calm, reasonable voice.

Frustration bit at Seth. How on earth was he supposed to protect Jess when he couldn't even tell where the danger was coming from?

Why not ask God?

No longer shocked by such thoughts, he paused.

Fine. God, please help me protect Jessie.

It was amazing, the sense of release that came with the thought. Huh. Maybe there was something to all this praying stuff, after all.

"Seth, we can do nothing at the moment. Get some more sleep, and after we take care of the chores and eat breakfast, I will help you look again."

Sighing, Seth gave in. What else could he do?

"I think even if you have been found, you are safe here, *jah*? The dogs will keep strangers away from the house. Jess is on the second floor. I do not believe anyone can get into her room without us knowing about it."

And with that, he had to be satisfied. Reluctantly, he went back into his room, knowing going back to sleep was impossible. Dragging a chair to the window, he sat, keeping watch.

Seth left his room, tucking the clean shirt that had been left for him into his trousers. Levi's, he assumed. Good thing the Amish fellow was about his size. He followed the soft voices speaking in Pennsylvania Dutch to the kitchen.

He braked as he entered the large room. There were a whole lot more people than he had been expecting. Mr. Miller came in the door, stomping his boots as he crossed to the table. He was followed by two younger men. Seth guessed their ages to be mid-to-late teens. A girl of around ten was near the counter with her mother. An older girl stood directly behind her. She didn't spare

Seth a glance as he entered, intent on fixing her sister's hair. Neither girl wore a prayer *kapp*, although they were fully dressed in every other way.

The rest of the room's occupants waved greetings at him as he came to a clumsy halt. None of them showed any surprise at the sight of him, so they had probably all been made aware of their guests.

Speaking of the guests... Seth felt someone at his shoulder, and knew without turning that it was Jess. He cast his eyes over his shoulder. His breath caught as he met her clear hazel eyes. The night's sleep seemed to have done her good. Her eyes were bright, and there was color in her cheeks.

She doesn't know. The sheer cheekiness of the smile she tossed at him told him that she was completely unaware that her attacker might have found them. Now was not the time to let her know. Too many people around. He would wait until they had more privacy.

Brushing past him, her fingers bumped into his hand. Electricity jolted through him. Her startled eyes met his. So she felt it, too. His fingers twitched.

Not. Going. To. Happen.

Distance, dude. Distance.

Giving her what he hoped was a nonchalant smile, he returned his focus to the Millers.

The door opened and Levi stomped in, his movements nearly identical to those of his father. He gave a small shake of his head at Seth. The pit of his stomach dropped. The message was clear. Levi had found no more trace of their early morning visitor.

"The mare is lame this morning, Dat. Her left front leg seems to be paining her," Levi announced.

"Would you like me to look at her for you?"

Seth blinked. He was a bit cowed surrounded by the large family. But Jess? She looked completely at ease, even though she was back in her dirty clothes from the day before. Maybe no one here was her size.

Levi ducked his head at Jess. "*Jah*. I did not see you. But I would like you to look at her."

Mr. Miller opened his mouth. He's going to object, Seth thought. But Levi cut him off.

"She knows more about horses than either of us, Dat."

Seth held his breath. If he went with her, then maybe that would be the opportunity to tell Jess about the trespasser. If she became emotional, there would be fewer eyes to see. He knew her well enough that she would hate others to see her in a weak moment.

"It is time to eat." Martha smoothly moved between the two men. Perfect timing. Seth wiped his mouth on his sleeve, hiding the smile that threatened to erupt at Martha's obvious intervention. Out of the corner of his eye, Jess mimicked his movement.

"Will you join us for breakfast?" Levi waved an arm toward the wooden table. Still off-balance, Seth waited until Jess sat, before placing himself at her side. Only when he was beside her did he remember his decision to distance himself. It didn't matter that he had meant emotional distance. Sitting so close to her was like putting a cookie jar in front of a child with a sweet tooth.

"Jessica, you are feeling better this morning, *jah*?" Martha asked.

Silence.

Frowning, Seth turned to Jess. It wasn't like Jess to be rude and ignore her hostess. Jess met his gaze, a puzzled wrinkle creasing her brow. Adorable. Mentally shaking his head, Seth repeated the question, signing.

Rich color flooded her cheeks.

"Oh! I'm so sorry, Mrs. Miller! I didn't hear you," her mortified face whipped around to meet the older woman's understanding gaze.

"I understand. I forgot to get your attention before I spoke. You are *gut*?"

"Yes, ma'am. I am feeling well today."

Martha brought a heaping plate of pancakes to the table. Seth's mouth watered as the aroma hit his nose. Closing his eyes, he inhaled deeply. Then his eyes popped open again as his stomach growled. Loud.

The children covered their mouths, but he still heard the snickers. Grinning, he shrugged. Well, now everyone knew he was hungry.

He was scooping a large bite of pancake dripping with warm maple syrup in his mouth when Jess raised her arm suddenly, knocking his food off his fork. It landed with a sticky slurp on his clean shirt. Grabbing the cloth napkin, he removed the mess, scrubbing at the spot, aware that he was making it worse. Finally giving up, he placed his napkin back on the table.

Jess was most likely wanting to crawl under the table with embarrassment, he mused. He turned to face her, prepared to make a joke of the accident. The joke died on his lips. Jess was rocking in her seat, her eyes darting from person to person. Actually, she was looking from face to face, zeroing in on their mouths as they talked.

Her panicked eyes caught his. He knew what she was going to say even before she signed it.

"My battery died. I can't hear."

Perfect. That was just great.

Because they needed one more challenge in their bid to survive.

Jess tried to remember when she had changed her battery last. Yesterday morning. Her batteries always lasted longer than that. What a time to get a bum battery!

She was trying to read lips so fast her vision was strained. If this continued, she would have a headache before lunch.

When Levi stood to go to the barn and look at the lame horse, she shoved her chair back and stood with more alacrity than grace. Belatedly, she remembered her manners. Heat seared her cheeks as she paused to thank her hostess.

"Thank you, Mrs. Miller. Breakfast was delicious."

"You're welcome, Jess. We are glad you decided to come to us."

Frustrated, Jess watched her hostess's mouth move, unable to decipher the rest of the words. A wave caught her attention. Discreetly, Seth signed, keeping his hands low. "She said you are like family."

A lump clogged her throat. Jess had felt bereft of family since her brother died. Just knowing that Rebecca's family accepted her touched her more than she could say. Again, the Lord blessed her when she needed it. Unable to reply without tearing up, she smiled and nodded before following Levi, aware that Seth had risen and joined them. Tension knotted her neck muscles as they walked to the barn. The way the men kept constant surveillance made her feel squirrely. By the time they reached the barn, she half expected someone to jump out at them. Men!

Jess fell in love with the mare Levi led her to the second she saw her. She was a chestnut thoroughbred, and stood about sixteen hands. The mare's legs weren't swollen, so that was good. She leaned down to feel the legs. No extra heat. Also good. The mare stood quietly while she examined her, not even protesting when Jess lifted her leg to look at the hoof. When she moved the horse to look at her gaits, the animal moved without pampering one limb over another.

"What a sweet girl," she crooned. The horse nudged her with her nose. "I can't see any problems. My guess is that she stepped on a rock or something, and it bothered her for a few steps. Nothing permanent. Keep an eye on her for the next day or so, just in case."

That done, she figured they would head back to the house. As it was Sunday, the family might have plans to visit family or neighbors. Now that the animals had been tended to, there was no more work that they would do.

So she was somewhat startled when Seth laid a gentle hand on her shoulder, holding her back.

"Jess, there's a situation you should know about before we go," Seth signed.

"What situation?" Her stomach started to hurt, the way it always did when she was scared.

"Early this morning, the dogs woke the two of us," he indicated Levi and himself, "and I saw someone running behind the barn. I don't know who it was. It might have nothing to do with us, but I thought you should know."

"You think we've been found." It wasn't a question.

And if Seth believed it, she believed it, too. He was observant, and had seen enough to know how serious their situation was.

Nor did Seth try to sugarcoat things. All her life, people had tried to shield her from bad news. It was something of a relief to meet someone who didn't try to keep information from her. Even if it was unpleasant information.

"So what you're saying is someone could be watching us right now?"

Seth nodded. Levi merely shrugged, a skeptical expression on his face. He apparently didn't feel they were in danger here. But as long as Seth did, she would assume the same.

"What do we do?" *Calm. We need to stay calm.* She repeated the words in her mind over and over.

Levi spoke. She was relieved when Seth signed, interpreting for her. It was exhausting to try and read Levi's lips.

"Mam and Dat will go visiting today. My brothers were out courting last night, so they will remain at home today. I had planned on visiting my girl today. If you need me, I could stay here."

"Oh, no! I don't want to interrupt your plans." She replied. Then curiosity got the better of her. "You have a girl?"

Seth sent her a glare, which she ignored. Yes, she was being nosy. But she had never known Levi to go courting before.

She almost relented when he shifted uncomfortably. "Yes, I have a girl. We are getting to know each other."

"Then you must go and see her. Seth and I can stay here out of the way. We have plenty of information we need to sort through. And plenty of suspects to consider. I'm going back and forth about whether or not I think Lisa and Bob Harvey could be guilty."

"Lisa and Bob Harvey? My girl cleans house for several *Englisch* families. The Harveys are one of them."

Jess's mouth dropped open. So did Seth's. Any plans to stay quietly tucked safe and sound at the Miller house fled. A golden opportunity had just been handed to them. She for one didn't want to waste it.

Seth apparently agreed. "We would very much like to talk with your girlfriend. Do you think she would agree?"

There was a brief hesitation. It might have been her imagination, but she knew it wasn't. It was one thing to allow them to enter his family's home. Quite another to introduce them to his girlfriend. If she remembered what Rebecca had told her correctly, dating couples didn't officially tell their families until a marriage proposal had been made. Although everyone knew.

Slowly, Levi nodded.

"*Jah*. I do not know if she will talk with you. She's shy. But you are my sister's oldest friend. I don't believe you are in danger here. But if someone is after you, it would be right to help." Levi's stern expression softened. "But you should not go dressed like you are now."

"I don't have anything else with me."

"*Jah*, but Rebecca left most of her clothes when she left. You could wear those."

She blinked. Wasn't there some kind of rule against what he was suggesting?

"You want us to dress Plain?"

Confirmation never hurt.

"*Jah*. I think it the best way. I think it would be safer for Laura if your enemy didn't recognize you."

Her heart softened. "Levi, I don't know how to thank you."

A casual shrug lifted his shoulders. "We will leave when you are ready. And when we come home tonight…"

"No," Seth interrupted.

"No?" Maybe she had read the single word that fell from Seth's lips wrong. No was such a small word. And there were other English words that looked the same. Like *toe*. Or *lo*. Both were quite a stretch.

He flicked his gaze toward her. It was filled with tenderness. And regret. Her breath got stuck in her lungs. This was either going to be very good, or very bad. Riveted, she gulped as he started to speak, signing for her benefit.

"I'm sorry, Jess. I know that you are among friends here. And Levi, we appreciate all that your family has done for us. Is still doing for us. But I know I saw someone this morning and I firmly believe that they were here for Jess and me. I doubt the person will go after your family, because they have nothing to do with this. And anyone who lives in the area knows the Amish community wouldn't go to the police to solve their problems. But if he or she recognizes Jess at your house, someone else might get hurt. So I think the best plan would be to let us talk with Laura, then help us find shelter for the night. You can pick us up tomorrow on your way to work so we can use the phone."

Her heart heavy, Jess agreed.

Levi did not. He started to argue. Before he could get

too far, though, his mother called him in to the house to assist her.

"This isn't finished," Seth waited for her to walk out of the stall, then he relatched it.

Jess held her tongue. Hopefully, their discussion with Levi's girlfriend would provide answers. They were out of options.

TEN

Jess was ready to crawl out of her own skin. She just knew someone was watching them. Her shoulder blades twitched under the plain blue dress, feeling a stare boring holes in her back. Her hand trembled, itching to reach up and adjust the white prayer *kapp* she had placed on her head. Resisting the urge was difficult.

With each step she took she braced herself for the bullet she expected to pierce her skin. It was a toss-up whether her inability to hear was a pro or a con at the moment. Did she want to hear a gunshot and know that death was coming if there was no escape?

Think of how Rebecca walks, she reminded herself. Concentrating on taking quick, gentle steps like her friend helped take her mind off the eminent danger. After all, she was wearing Rebecca's old dress and shoes. Might as well pretend to be her for the next fifty feet or so.

Closer. Closer.

Almost there.

The last few steps she had to force herself not to run. The questionable safety of the buggy beckoned to her. Seth stepped up beside her to offer her a hand into the buggy. She avoided his eyes. Not because she was upset with him. She wasn't. Both he and Levi were doing their best to keep her safe. Levi had even gone as far as raiding the family's clothes to locate an appropriate disguise for her and Seth. Her fear was that if she risked raising her head, her attacker would get a look at her face.

Jess didn't know much about the attacker. One thing she was absolutely certain of, however, was that it was someone she knew. Or at least someone who knew her. How else could they have known where she'd go to take shelter on this side of the flooded creek? That's why it had been so crucial to mimic Rebecca's mannerisms. To become someone else for even a few minutes.

Without needing to be told she moved to the back of the buggy, sliding into one corner on the dark gray bench inside. Levi had cautioned her not to let her head be seen out of the side windows. It meant she had to sit at an awkward angle, but she didn't care. If staying alive meant she had to twist herself up like a pretzel, then that's what she would do.

The buggy shook as Seth took a seat in the back with her. She had to smile. He looked very uncomfortable in Levi's old hat and plain clothes. The buggy moved forward with a lurch, and they were both pitched against the back wall.

"I will never complain about how small my car is," she signed to Seth.

Only the tiniest twitch at the corners of his mouth told her he was amused. She was getting good at reading his eyes, though. They were warm and full of caring. But guarded.

"I'm sorry that I put you in such danger," he said.

He thought he'd put her in danger?

"I think you have that backward. I'm the one who convinced you to bring me to that party in the first place, even though I knew someone was out to get me. So technically, I put you in danger." She rested her hands in her lap, waiting.

He tilted his head back against the wall, but kept his eyes slanted toward her.

"I wasn't really that hard to convince," he signed. "I thought you would be safer at my uncle's house than in your house all by yourself."

For some odd reason, that statement struck her as funny. She started to snicker, covering her mouth with her hand, trying to hold the gasps and giggles in. How much she succeeded, she had no way of knowing. Not much, she guessed, as his shoulders shook.

"It's not your job to protect me, you know," she signed after she had finally managed to control herself.

Uh, oh. She would know that stubborn look anywhere. And if she wasn't mistaken, her words had offended him. Well, that certainly hadn't been her intent. How was she to know he was so sensitive?

"I'm not helping you because it's my job," he told her, his signs quick, jerky. Definitely irritated. "I'm helping you because you're my friend. And friends are supposed to look out for each other."

Wow. Friends with Seth Travis. She had known they were growing closer, but to be let into the circle of his friends was humbling.

Uh, oh. His face tightened. She hadn't responded. Bad move.

Okay, then. She needed to make this right. How?

"I'm sorry I offended you. I am glad you consider

me your friend. I was afraid that you considered me an obligation. You know, as if you had to atone for high school, or something stupid like that."

A stillness came over him. Something she had said had struck a chord. Good or bad, she wasn't sure. The expression on his face changed. He looked...vulnerable?

"Whether you know it or not, I do need to make amends. And not just to you. I allowed my arrogance and my bad relationship with my father turn me into someone I'm not proud of."

He shifted, turning his face away. Jess held her breath, waiting. She could sense the struggle inside him. *Please, Lord, help him.*

Shifting again, she saw his chest rise and fall with a sigh. "I don't know if you remember my friend, Melanie?"

She nodded. In her mind, she could picture the pretty brunette.

"After I broke up with Trish, Mel and I started dating. After a few years, we even got engaged. But then I let my father turn me against her. I abandoned her when she needed me most. She ended up spending four years of her life in jail. And she was innocent. How do I reconcile that?" He signed, meeting her gaze, his own anguished. "I mean, we're friends again, but I don't understand it. How she could forgive me. How her husband could let me be a part of their lives. And even my sister, she doesn't hold a grudge toward my father. Even though he was a jerk to her mom."

He may not understand, but she was pretty sure that she did.

"They're Christians, aren't they? Melanie and your sister?"

Caution entered his face, but he nodded.

"They forgave you because it's what their faith, their love for God, tells them to do. Just like He forgives us, when we ask Him." She sighed at his closed expression. "Seth, no matter what you have done, He wants to forgive you. No one loves you more than God. And He is waiting for you to trust Him."

"How do you know?" His hands were clumsy. He was getting emotional, even though his face didn't show it. "I have done so many things I'm not proud of. What if I fail again?"

She couldn't help it. She rolled her eyes. "Please. Like you have a monopoly on failing those around you? It's called being human. We all fail. And you may be your father's son, but you have been very brave and heroic since we met again."

He sneered, apparently thinking she was being sarcastic.

"Seriously, Seth. You have saved my life half a dozen times. And you have not abandoned me. That means a lot to me."

She had shocked him. She could tell by the way he kept raising his hands, then setting them down again. He didn't quite know how to respond to that.

"I guess." Pause. "You know what the saddest thing about my father is?"

She shook her head, not really knowing if he wanted a response. "He's had so many affairs that he has several children. Not just me and Maggie. One is in jail. One is dead. And I have another sister, although I have no idea where she is. Yet for all those kids, not one of them is close to him. Maggie tolerates him, but she doesn't trust him."

"What about the child who is…lost?" Should she have asked?

"Her name is Carrie. She's a teenager being raised by her older half sister. I have never even met her, though I want to. It hurts knowing I may never meet her."

"Maybe you will. Someday."

He shrugged. "Yeah, maybe. Maggie and I have tried to find her. But she moves around a lot. Anyway, I figure if I don't get involved with anyone, then I can't hurt them, either."

And there it was. The warning to keep her distance. But she knew it was too late. She swallowed, wanting to cry. But would she be crying for Seth, who was choosing to shut life out and live in solitude? Or would her tears be for herself, knowing the man she was falling for was placing himself out of her reach?

He couldn't believe he had gone on like that. He never talked about his relationship with his father. Or about Carrie. She was like some deep dark secret in his family. The only person he had ever mentioned her to was Maggie.

Until now.

What was it about Jess? She was way too easy to talk to. Getting him to go all emo like that. Not cool.

Except he didn't feel like a dork. Instead, it was like a little bit of the pressure that had been building inside of him had been released and now there was more room to breathe.

Unfortunately, there was also more to think about. Her words about God swirled around in his brain, so fast he could barely keep track of them.

God loved him. Did He?

God would forgive him—how did she know?

The buggy lurched again, breaking into his thoughts. Seth pushed his hand down on the seat to brace himself. The clop, clop sound made by the hooves or the horse changed. Sharpened.

"Are we on the paved road now?" he called up to Levi.

"*Jah*. We will be on the paved road for the next mile until we reach the Hostetlers' road."

Paved road. That meant more traffic. Was that good or bad? They were more out in the open, true. Also true was the fact that there was more of a chance that there would be witnesses if anyone came after them. And it would be made even more difficult if the person coming after them was on foot still.

Route 89 twisted like a thick, lazy snake through the outer edges of Spartansburg. Seth could hear the hum of an engine behind them. Even knowing that their hunter was most likely on foot didn't eliminate the urge to peek through the small window in the back of the buggy. If he stretched upward just an inch or two he could get a look at what was happening behind them. Not that he had any intention of doing that. But the temptation tickled his mind again and again.

The engine revved again, and moved to the side. The buggy swayed. The vehicle was rushing past. Good.

Jess reached across the space dividing them and grabbed his hand. Her face was white.

She couldn't hear what was happening, although he had no doubt she had felt the buggy move.

"A car is passing," he signed with his free hand.

She nodded, but her hand remained in his. The warmth of her slim hand seeped into his skin. When was the last time someone had truly touched him so intimately, with so much trust? His protective shell cracked. His gaze was pulled down to their joined hands. They looked right together.

No.

Tightening his resolve, he pulled his hand from hers and used it to scratch his opposite shoulder so as not to hurt her feelings. Dipping his head so he could see her expression, he sighed. *Jerk. You hurt her anyway.*

Jess folded her hands together in her lap and leaned her head against the side of the buggy, closing her eyes with a sigh. Yeah, he got that message loud and clear. Conversation was done. He'd been shut out as definitely as if she had slammed a door in his face. And locked it.

Fair enough—it was what he deserved.

Discomfort shrouded the remainder of the journey.

Bumps and creaks announced their return to a gravel road. The sharp clop of hooves hitting pavement softened.

Beside him, Jess sat straight up.

"Do I smell sawdust? That means we're close to the sawmill! We're almost there!" She reached out and shook Seth's arm. Then just as quickly pulled her hand back.

Way to go, Travis. She's really offended.

But she gave no other sign of being offended. Instead, she bounced on the seat like a small child. A chuckle slipped past his lips. He didn't even try to hold it in, knowing she wouldn't hear it. *Man, there's that dimple again.*

"We are at the Hostetlers' house now. I'm going to take the buggy back to the garage. Laura's *dat* will not approve of you wearing Plain clothes. You can change in the barn."

With a quick flick of his wrists, Levi steered the horse into the driveway. Seth angled his head so he could view the large white house as they drove past it. The drive veered to the right, and they moved into the barn. The smell of hay and animal waste assaulted his nostrils.

Ugh. He liked horses and enjoyed riding, but could do without the odor that accompanied them. He would never make a good farmer. Not that he had any interest in giving up his job as a paramedic. The sudden image of Jess out cold on the freezer floor filled his mind. A single, sharp shake banished the image.

Levi halted the buggy and jumped down. "I will go find Laura now before the family becomes curious. There is a room in the back you can take turns and change in."

Without a backward look he hurried from the barn. It was up to Seth to jump down and lend Jess a hand. He grinned at the annoyed frown creasing her brow. She was such an independent woman; it probably galled her to need help from the buggy. Wearing Rebecca's dress, though, she didn't have much of a choice. Which was probably why she didn't complain. As she settled her hand on his shoulder, he found he had no wish to complain, either. What would it be like to be the recipient of such simple intimacies with her on a daily basis?

"What's going on?" Jess asked. He couldn't believe he had forgotten to sign what was happening to her. Just one more example of how he was the wrong man for her. A worthy man would have remembered to include her in the conversation.

"Stop that!"

Jess's voice slashed like a whip, startling him out of his maudlin thoughts. Planting her fists on her slim hips, she faced him. The demure, modest Amish dress and *kapp* contrasted with the tense, stubborn line of her jaw and the fire flashing from her eyes.

"Huh? Stop what?"

"You're blaming yourself for something. I didn't realize at first what that expression on your face meant. But now I recognize it. It's the same look you wear right before you apologize for some imagined wrong you've done."

Oh, yeah? This was good.

"You can't seriously be telling me that I haven't done anything I need to apologize for."

He got an exaggerated eye roll for his trouble.

"Not since high school. And I forgave that one."

His mouth went dry, making him need to swallow before he could speak. And then he found that he couldn't think of anything to say. Because her forgiveness left him feeling…what? Free? Light? Both, he decided.

Remembering her question, and the fact that Levi would be returning soon with Laura, he repeated the plan. Jess nodded, leaning back inside the buggy to grab her rolled up bundle of clothes.

"Catch!" she called out, hefting his own bundle toward him. Winking, she sashayed back to the room to change.

Seth watched her go, suddenly aware that he was grinning like a loon.

But as she closed the door, the smile slipped from his face. He hadn't yet told her that they would have to remain here overnight. Nor had he convinced Levi yet. But if they returned back to the Millers' house, he couldn't shake the feeling that they would be putting the Miller family in danger. It was hard to believe that anyone could have followed them to the Hostetler house.

In spite of that, a chill swept up his spine. He wished more than anything that he could take this danger away from her, make himself the target instead. He'd be happy to stand in the killer's sights if it meant that Jess was safe.

"Your turn."

Pivoting to face Jess, he filled his lungs with barn air, stunned as the truth slapped him in the face. This woman, this brave, fierce woman, challenged and inspired him. And he was falling in love with her.

But that didn't mean he was free to pursue her. He couldn't take the chance. He had too many memories of his father failing his family. Memories of the tears his mother had tried to hide from him. Of the forced smiles she would hold on her face for him.

Of his mother fighting for her life while his father wined and dined some woman across town.

All his adult life he had struggled to be different from his father. And he believed he had succeeded. But Jess was too precious to take the chance.

He would protect her. He would risk his life for her, wouldn't even hesitate. And then, he would walk away.

Even if it killed him.

ELEVEN

Seth paced back and forth in front of the barn door, his hands knotted together behind his back. How long did it take to run up to the house and back? He and Jess had been waiting for Levi's return for nearly an hour.

"What if something happened to him?"

Jess's question echoed his own fears.

"He's fine," he asserted.

A slapping noise alerted him to people approaching. Levi? Maybe…or maybe not. Waving Jess to get back into the shadows, he grabbed a shovel and slunk low against the barn wall. Wincing as a splinter wedged itself into his arm, he concentrated on the door. If anyone other than Levi or his friends entered, he wanted to be ready. His stomach clenched. Even if it was his aunt. Willa might look like a harmless flake, but he knew that she was a dead shot. He had accompanied the Taylors to the shooting range twice a month for the last five years. The question wasn't whether or not Willa had the skill. She did. No, the question was whether she was cold blooded enough to pull the trigger on a human being.

And if she'd pulled the trigger on Vic Horn.

The barn door shuddered. Someone on the other side

had grasped the handle and was sliding it open. Light sliced through the crevice in a narrow beam, increasing as the opening widened. It pierced the shadows, leaving Jess and Seth vulnerable.

He gripped the shovel, hefting it to his shoulder.

Then let it drop as Levi sauntered through the opening. The Amish gentleman reared back, mouth dropping open. After a startled second, he flashed a grin at Seth. A petite woman stepped through the door after him. Seeing Seth, she dropped her eyes.

Feeling foolish, Seth leaned the offending tool against the wall before shoving his hands in his pockets.

"This is my Laura," Levi introduced his girlfriend, pride ringing in his voice.

A sharp twinge of envy pricked Seth. How he wished he could say, "This is my Jess!"

Don't go there. It didn't do any good to dwell on what he could never have.

"Levi wanted me to talk to you about my work," Laura murmured.

But she didn't want to. That was clear. The Amish were deeply committed to not interfering in the affairs of others, particularly those outside of their community. Sharing information about her employers—information that might lead to them facing criminal charges— must be incredibly difficult for her. Seth wondered how long Levi had needed to talk to her, to persuade her to come out and talk with a couple of strange *Englischers*. His gratitude to the man increased. That must have been awkward, especially considering how he felt about Laura.

Seth repeated her comment in sign to Jess.

"Hi, Laura," Jess greeted the woman, her voice low

and calm. Almost as if she were approaching a skittish animal. So he wasn't the only one who sensed her concern. "We're very grateful that you consented to help us. It means a lot."

Laura flicked her narrowed gaze between them. Suspicion poured off her, but she nodded her head cautiously. "Levi says you are in danger. And that you are his sister's oldest friend. Also, I know that the people I work for are *Englisch*, so they are still under your law."

"That's right." Seth responded, making sure to use his voice and sign simultaneously.

He was unsure how to begin the discussion. Turned out, he didn't need to. Jess took the bull by the horns and dove in.

"Okay, here's the situation. We were stranded at Ted and Willa Taylor's house Friday night. Someone there was trying to harm us, and we believe whoever it was has followed us. This is all connected to my brother, who died in suspicious circumstances after being accused of stealing money."

She stopped and drew in a deep breath.

Laura tilted her head, pursing her mouth into a tight little bow.

"I am sorry that your brother died. I am confused, though. I do not understand how my employers are connected with your problems."

Seth broke in. "The Harveys were at my uncle's house, and they were seen talking with someone who ended up dead." He went on to explain about the run-ins they'd had since arriving at the Taylors' house.

"I'm not sure how they are connected with Cody's organization. What was the name of it, Jess?"

"Racing to the Rescue," Jess replied.

"Oh!" Laura's hand flashed up to cover her mouth. "I know of this organization!"

He had never actually seen anyone do a double take, but Levi sure did one now. His normally calm face was comical as his mouth dropped open and his eyes bugged in his face.

"You have heard of it? I know of it because I am familiar with Jessica and her brother. How did you hear of it?"

Laura cast her gaze down, then flicked it up again. "About six months ago, I was cleaning the Harveys' house. I was in the living room, dusting. Mr. Harvey arrived home, unexpectedly." She licked her lips and shifted her weight. "I was surprised. I leave before suppertime, so he never comes home while I am there. Mr. and Mrs. Harvey went into another room, the den, and I could hear them arguing. I can't recall the whole conversation, but I do remember that it had something to do with a racehorse they owned. Someone had accused them of abusing the horse. Mr. Harvey was afraid they would lose the horse and the money it had cost them. Or that they would go to prison. Mrs. Harvey was crying and carrying on something awful. She was afraid they would lose everything. I had never heard a grown woman take on so. I remember them talking about someone from Racing to the Rescue. They were scared. Real scared."

"Did you hear anything more? See anything?" Seth leaned toward her.

She backed up.

Whoa. Hold on man. Coming on a little too intense.

"Sorry. Didn't mean to startle you. Jess and I need something we can take to the police."

Moving closer to Laura, Levi glared at Seth.

"She will tell you what she knows. Give her time."

Time. The one thing they were running out of. Because even if they got back to LaMar Pond tomorrow, which he desperately hoped they would, there was still the small matter of some psychopath gunning for his girl. How was he supposed to keep her safe if they couldn't narrow down the field of suspects?

He had spent enough time with Dan and with Jace—Melanie's husband, who was also on the police force—to know that they needed solid evidence to go on if they were going to reopen the case of Cody's death. And if they reopened the case, who was to say that the killer wouldn't take her attacks on Jess up a notch? Just to get Jess out of the way.

Laura and Levi were holding a private conversation. Jess quirked one eyebrow at him, asking a question. He shrugged back. "They're talking Amish," he signed to her.

That sweet mouth curved in amusement, drawing his eyes to it. He wrenched them away, slipping two fingers beneath his suddenly too-tight collar to loosen it.

"It's called Pennsylvania Dutch," she signed, obviously unaware of the level of attraction he was fighting.

Another clue that they weren't meant for each other. Sometimes he was so sure she felt something for him, but other times, she didn't seem affected by his presence at all.

"There was something more," Laura stated.

Seth whipped his head around, even as his hands signed her response.

He waited. Tapped his foot.

Laura pressed her lips together and twisted her hands. Still Seth waited. Something brushed his arm. Jess moved forward, leaning in as her eyes bore into Laura's face. Probably trying to read Laura's lips instead of relying on Seth to relay the information. Poor Laura squirmed. He understood. Jess could be quite intense when she wanted something.

"A few minutes after they argued, Mr. Harvey left the den and ran into the living room with his arms full of papers. He threw them into the fireplace. When he looked around and saw me, he got real red and yelled at me to go work in another room. Mrs. Harvey apologized after he left. But I noticed something…he had dropped a couple of papers. Mrs. Harvey picked them up, and I saw her shove them into the top drawer of the china cabinet."

"Tell them the rest," Levi urged her.

"Mrs. Harvey has been taking shooting lessons this past year." The Amish girl raised her head and aimed a level glance at them. "She has shown me awards she has won at shooting contests."

"Seth," Jess breathed, her hand clutching at his arm.

"This might be what we need, Jess." Throwing his arm around her shoulders, he squeezed tightly, laughing softly when she squealed. The laughter died in his throat when he caught her eyes. The air between them hummed with electricity. He was sure that if he looked down at his arms, he would see the hairs standing on end. He removed his arm from her shoulders, but it didn't help. It took all his effort to pull his gaze from her. Facing Levi and Laura, he found them watching with curiosity. Levi's expression was sympathetic.

He knows, Seth thought. He knows how I feel about her. So much for stopping himself from falling for her. Too late.

He had fallen too deeply to extricate himself without pain. The most he could hope for was leaving without hurting her, as well.

She was breathless, light-headed. But wasn't sure why. Was it because they finally had something real to bring to the police? Or was it because of the tension flowing between her and Seth like a wave, connecting them?

A little of both, most likely.

She could tell that Seth didn't want to feel the connection. His face was tight, drawn. He had removed his arm so fast, it was as if lightning had struck it. Now he was clenching and unclenching his fists. Fine. Just fine. She should have learned her lesson by the way he reacted to a simple touch in the back of the buggy.

How long had Levi been gone? At their insistence, he had gone inside the house to visit with Laura. Leaving Jess and Seth alone.

Shifting back a step, she put distance between them, mentally and physically. By sheer force of will she kept her face blank. It was a true challenge. Inside, she fumed. *Give it to God,* she reminded herself, hating the way bitterness churned her emotions and thoughts. *Give Seth to God. Only He can help him.* Dragging in a deep breath, she sent a prayer up to God. Only then was she able to let go of the angst gnawing away at her mind.

It was time to get back to figuring out what had happened to Cody. Time to stop whoever was out to get her. And time to go back to her life. Alone.

When it was time for Levi to return home a couple of hours later, Seth stopped him.

"Levi...look, I appreciate all you are doing for us. I really do. But Jess and I, well, I don't think we should stay at your place tonight. It doesn't feel right, putting your family in danger."

Crossing his arms over his chest, Levi shook his head. "I do not agree. We saw no sign of anyone following us this morning. You need to trust *Gott*. He will protect you."

Seth set his feet apart and matched the Amish man, stare for stare.

Uh, oh. This could become ugly. Men. Why were they always so stubborn?

"Levi," Jess broke in. "I have to go with Seth on this one. I would feel guilty forever if something happened to anyone in your family because of me. I have already dragged Seth into my troubles."

She ignored Seth when he moved impatiently. If Seth was irritated, that was just too bad.

"Jessica, what is your other choice?" Levi asked slowly. Her heart softened. He was trying to make sure she could lip read him. She knew that even though his sister was deaf, Levi was uncomfortable signing. Felt it drew too much attention to himself. But he tried to find other ways to accommodate her and Rebecca. He was a good brother. Just like Cody had been. "You cannot go off on your own and spend a night in this man's company. Even if you are in danger. It would not be right."

A few more minutes were spent arguing. Levi and Seth were both unmovable in their stance.

"You have to go," Laura interrupted. "My *dat* will

not like it if you stay in his barn alone tonight. You go with Levi. You cannot stay here."

And it was settled.

Not that Jess was satisfied with the outcome. Neither was Seth. She could see worry etching deep lines in his forehead. Her fingers tingled with the desire to reach out and smooth the wrinkles away.

She slammed her hands into her pockets instead.

The short walk to the buggy was tense. By unspoken agreement, Seth and Levi sandwiched her between them. The blue sky had darkened to a heavy gray. She sniffed the air. More rain? Her heart sank at the thought. The clouds moving in had banished the sunlight, creating the perfect background for a horror story. Unfortunately, the horror story was her life. Again, her shoulder blades twitched, as she imagined someone watching them. Without her hearing aids to give her some clue about what was going on around her she was relying on her vision, eyes in constant motion, side to side. Was that a movement? Was someone in the trees? Good grief. She was going to drive herself crazy.

Her neck soon started to ache from the way she'd been holding herself so stiffly. The urge to lengthen her strides was strong.

That wouldn't do. She forced herself to slow down. *Calm. Have to appear calm.*

Seth moved his head to gaze at her. He slowed, motioning her into the buggy ahead of him. As she moved past him, his hand snaked out and grabbed hers. Startled, she glanced up at him.

"Jessie, I won't let anything happen to you."

Jessie? Maybe she had read it wrong, but she didn't

think so. Blinking, she pushed back the moisture gathering in her eyes. It had been so long since anyone called her Jessie. Only her father ever had. But he was gone now. Everyone was gone. And the one man to make her feel alive didn't want her.

Straightening her shoulders, she pulled away from Seth. "I'm good."

He tilted his head and narrowed his eyes. Clearly, the man didn't believe her. Well, that was his problem. Ignoring him, she reached up and pulled herself into the buggy. Warmth crept up her cheeks as he grasped her elbow to assist her. Tingles swept up her arm from where he touched her.

"Thanks," she muttered.

If only she could hear her voice right now. Did it sound normal? She often read in the Christian romance novels she enjoyed that the heroine's voice sounded breathless when she was affected by the hero's presence. Did she sound breathless? She certainly felt that way. And was none too happy about it. The last thing she wanted was to give Seth the idea that she was attracted to him. Even if she was. Maybe she should stick to sign only until she had her aids back.

When they pulled up outside the Miller house, it was still quiet. The family hadn't returned from visiting for the day. Levi hopped down from his seat and went to unharness the horse. "I will put the horse in the back field for the night. Make yourself at home." Leading the horse, he disappeared around the corner.

"We might as well go in," Jess murmured. She made to jump out, but Seth pulled her back.

"Let me go first."

She rolled her eyes, but let her macho companion lead the way. Suddenly, she remembered what he had said before about failing those he cared about and realized that his attitude wasn't macho. It was the sign of a brave man putting others' safety ahead of his own. She couldn't mock him for that. Her insides trembled as he stood clear outside, like a target. On purpose. She was about to call him back when he nodded and climbed back inside.

"I don't see anyone, but I'm not sure I trust that. I was sure I saw someone this morning, even if Levi and his dad disagree. How fast can you move into the house?"

"I can move very fast in these…oh, no!" Her hands covered her mouth. Seth raised his eyebrows, waiting. "Seth, we left our Amish clothes back at Laura's barn. Anyone watching us will know who we are."

He shrugged. "Yeah, I thought of that a few minutes ago, but there was no way we could go back. I had the feeling we had all but worn out our welcome there. Not to mention the fact that anyone noticing us signing to each other will figure it out. You ready?"

No.

"Yes."

Clambering down, they started running to the house. Seth grabbed her hand and dragged her to match his quicker pace.

A chunk of driveway blew up in front of her. Someone was shooting at them. A second shot hit the front post of the porch. A golf ball–sized hole appeared, the smooth white paint and wood beneath it disappearing in a puff of smoke.

Racing together they ran up the steps. Two steps before the door, Seth lurched forward, slamming against the wall next to the door.

A dark red stain spread out, covering the top of his left arm.

Seth had been shot.

TWELVE

Jess yanked the door open, using her body as a wedge. She reached out and tugged at Seth, intent on bringing him into the house for safety. He staggered toward her, his face pale, but seeming otherwise alert and coherent. Once they were both inside, she slammed the door behind them.

Oh, no. Levi. Just as she was wondering how to get to him, the floor beneath her feet vibrated from the pounding of approaching footsteps. Whirling in terror, she braced herself to face a monster with a gun. Instead she saw her friend charging inside, his straw hat flying off his head in his haste.

"Are you well?" Levi shouted.

"Seth has been shot. I don't know what to do."

Seth tugged at her hand. She turned to see him sinking into one of the wooden chairs from the kitchen table. A chair far from the kitchen window, she noted. Which meant that he couldn't be seen from a distance. Not unless someone walked right up to the house. She shuddered.

"Easy, Jess," he said, closing his eyes briefly. "It's just my arm. Nothing serious. I need your help though. I can't do this alone."

"Anything," she declared. And it was true. She would do anything to help this man.

"Help me get this shirt off."

He had already unbuttoned the flannel shirt, revealing a dark black-and-gold football T-shirt underneath. She stepped over to maneuver the shirt inch by inch down his injured arm. He tensed beneath her fingertips when she moved the material over the wound. She bit her lip hard, and blinked back the tears that sprouted, clouding her vision. Using her own sleeve, she wiped her face, then continued working.

After what felt like a lifetime, the shirt was off. Rolling up his T-shirt sleeve, she saw the wound for the first time. The sight of the blood coating his muscled arm made her dizzy. She refused to give in to her weakness. Not when he needed her.

Seth reached over and chucked her under the chin with his good hand. "It's not that bad. Honest." He smiled, but it was weak.

"Really?"

"Really. It looks bad because it bled a lot, but look. It's just a graze. If we went outside, I think there's a good chance we'd find the bullet lodged in the side of the house. When we get to a phone, we'll have to remember to tell the police to search for it."

Moving her head closer, she inspected the wound. Sure enough, there was no hole. The bullet wasn't inside him. And the bleeding seemed to have slowed down significantly already. She sighed. And for some odd reason, wanted to cry again.

She held off until she had finished bandaging Seth's arms using the cloths that Levi had brought them.

As she stood back to inspect her handiwork, the horror of the situation sank into her soul. Someone had shot Seth. Aiming for her, no doubt, and missed. Unable to help herself, she glanced down at the flannel shirt lying on the kitchen floor. The sight of the jagged hole in the material, surrounded by a bloody stain, was the final straw. She began to shake. Her mind urged her to flee the room, to hide her tears, but her legs wouldn't obey. Instead, all she could do was bring her shaking hands up to cover her face.

Warm arms embraced her, cradling her close. She felt Seth's breath in her hair, and knew he was probably talking to her. Whether he was whispering words of comfort or telling her to stop being a baby, she neither knew nor cared. Both hands grasped at his shirt as she buried her face in the soft fabric and sobbed. Sobbed so hard her chest hurt, for what felt like hours.

Finally, the tears trickled to a halt. She grew aware of her surroundings again. Mortified, she realized that she had lost total control in front of Seth. All she wanted to do now was go and hide.

Releasing her death grip, she backed out of the comforting circle of the strong arms holding her. Her movement met with slight resistance as he tightened his hold, just for a second, before letting her go.

As she moved away, she couldn't help but see the humongous wet spot on the front of his shirt. Mortification raced back in a warm rush up her neck and cheeks.

A gentle hand moved to her chin. Her breath stilled. Seth tilted her face up and studied her. His expression was torn. Almost tortured. She saw compassion, yearning and regret all mixed. The yearning won out as Seth's mouth moved. Her name. That's all he said before his head descended. His lips met hers and her lids fluttered shut.

Everything else faded. As he lifted his head, she could feel his breath stir across her lips before he kissed her again. Deeper and longer.

A quaking started deep in her soul. Now was not the time to explore her feelings. And yet she couldn't bring herself to pull away. Not when this kiss felt like it was mending every bruised and battered strand of her heart.

The kiss ended as gently as it had begun. Seth placed his forehead against hers.

Jess had no idea how long they had stayed like that. Vibrations under her feet indicated Levi was coming back into the room. Was he walking that heavily on purpose, giving them warning before he entered? The thought that he might have seen them kissing should have embarrassed her, but it didn't. No. A single kiss may not alter the fact that both Jess and Seth had issues to work out. And the odds were not in favor of a lasting relationship between them.

But she had no regrets.

That kiss had been a beautiful gift in a time of ugliness and fear. No matter what happened, she would always treasure it.

Seth wouldn't, though. She could already read the self-recriminations lurking in his face.

He had kissed her. Not once, but twice. And if he hadn't heard Levi's voice calling his name, he would have kissed her again!

To say he regretted giving in to the urge was a gross understatement. The kiss just made him want what he couldn't have. Walking away from her when all of this was over just became ten times harder.

Yeah, because it would have been so easy before.

Levi waved a note at them. "My *mam* and *dat* and the others decided to go visiting today. They will be staying overnight."

"Oh, I'm so glad!" Jess folded her hands beneath her chin, shooting a smile at Levi. Her lips trembled. "I would hate it if they came home while some maniac is out there shooting anything that moves."

Hardly anything, Seth mused, pressing his lips together. *Just you.* Of course, he would never point that out. No reason to scare her. But he had no doubt she would come to that conclusion on her own.

"I do not think anyone will shoot at Mam and Dat if you are not with them."

Thanks a lot, Mr. Sensitive. Seth released a sigh. Loudly.

Before Jess could start blaming herself, Seth tapped her shoulder.

"Come on," he said, nudging her, deliberately overlooking her stricken expression. "We've been still too long. We need to make sure the doors and windows are locked or barricaded. I don't think we can rely on only the dogs to keep us safe."

A sense of urgency pushed them into action. The lock on the back door was so worn, it was more for show. It would never withstand the pressure of someone trying to break in. Levi grabbed nails and two hammers. Seth took one and together they nailed the door shut to secure it. Seth shoved the hammer in his pocket and stepped back to inspect their work. Only a temporary fix, but hopefully it would be enough to keep them safe until they could figure out what else to do.

The window over the kitchen sink proved to be the most problematic. Not only was the locking mechanism pathetic, the window itself had no covering. Not even a decorative valance. Anyone could look in.

"Okay, Jess, Levi. I think we need to somehow cover this window. Maybe a towel. It will cut down on the light in the house, but we could use candles if we get desperate." His arm was aching. He knew he should be resting, but the safety of the others had to come first. Always.

Levi left the room to search for the items they needed. He returned a minute later and laid the towel and some candles on the table. Seth pulled the hammer they had used on the back door out of his pocket.

"Jess, you need to get back." They couldn't risk the shooter seeing her through the window and taking another shot. Her nod was unenthusiastic, to say the least, but at least she didn't object.

Light flashed briefly out the window. Then it was gone. Foreboding washed over him, sending trickles of unease into his mind. Leaning closer to the window, he narrowed his eyes. There it was again. Something in the trees was reflecting the sunlight.

"Get down!"

Even as he shouted at Levi, he caught Jess in his arms and dove to the ground with her, instinctively angling so he took the brunt of the impact as they hit the floor. He grunted in pain as she landed squarely on his injured arm.

CRASH.

The window shattered inward, spewing glass over them. A chunk of the kitchen wall splintered.

Jess screamed as the bullet made its home in the wall. Using his hands to indicate that she needed to keep low, Seth pushed himself to kneel.

Dogs barked outside the house, the bloodthirsty howls raising the hair on the back of his neck.

A second shot rang out. It lodged in the wall next to the first one. Kneeling on the ground between Jess and Levi, Seth's mouth went dry as he stared at the two bullets. If he hadn't looked out the window when he did, those bullets would have been lodged inside Jess and himself. It wasn't a coincidence that had caused the killer to miss them. God had protected them.

"Thank You, Jesus."

The prayer was sincere.

"Amen," Levi responded.

He shot a glance toward Jess. Her eyes were wide. She had read the prayer on his lips. Right now, all he saw was the trickle of blood on her cheek. The glass had struck her. It was a small cut, but to his mind it was still too much.

They knew exactly where the shooter was. Adrenalin spiked his heart rate. This could be their chance.

Maybe, if he drew the killer's attention, Jess could escape into town. But how?

How, indeed.

No cars. The buggy was out in the open and unhitched.

The horses, though...

"The horses. You can ride bareback, right?"

Okay, she might deny it later, but that was definitely a snort of disgust at the ridiculousness of the question. Jess's nose wrinkled and her lip curled in disdain. "Please."

"I'll take that as a yes. Levi?"

"*Jah*. But where will we go?"

"And," Jess drew the word out, her eyes narrowed on him, "how will we get out of here without drawing more fire?"

"We won't. You and Levi will." As she opened her mouth to protest, he continued quickly, signing to make sure he was understood. "We know that the shooter is out front. I will go out the front door, and make a run for it. Hopefully, the shooter will aim for me. I'm fast, so I have a good chance. You and Levi will slip out a window in the back. Head for the horses in the field, and try to ride to town. Find a phone and call the police. And if there are no phones, at least find someone who can help us."

Levi shook his head. "I should go out the front door. This is my house."

"No. You'll want to make for Spartansburg, and I don't know that area well. Or the people. You can find help quicker."

That, and he didn't know if Levi was a quick runner. There was a chance that he'd be shot before he stepped three feet out the door.

"Most people won't be out on a Sunday. Only in emergencies."

"I would think this qualifies as an emergency," Seth muttered.

"*Jah*," Levi frowned. "This morning Dat and I thought you had imagined the person in the woods. There didn't seem to be a reason to rush out and use a phone on a Sunday. Tomorrow seemed soon enough."

Seth read what the other man didn't say. If they had believed him, maybe none of this would have happened.

"No use second-guessing. It is what it is."

Jess. Always practical.

A dog growled right outside the door. It was joined by a second one. The barking resumed. One of the dog's yelped in pain. And it was too close to the house.

A new aroma wafted in the window.

Smoke. Something was on fire.

"Seth!"

He nodded. "I smell it. Something's burning. Stay low."

The smoke started to drift in the air. It formed a hazy cloud.

"It's coming from the back door." Levi stated. His voice was calm, in contrast to the ashen cast on his face.

On hands and knees, Seth crawled to the sink. There were several damp clothes hanging on it. He handed them to Jess and Levi. He grabbed a third. It wasn't as damp as he would have liked, but would have to do. Indicating that they needed to hold it over their mouths and noses, he began crawling toward the next room. His injured arm throbbed. Gritting his teeth, he kept crawling. He'd rather deal with a little pain than be dead. Entering the living room, he saw immediately that the smoke was thicker. It hung in the air like a wet blanket. Heavy.

He stopped.

Because he had no idea where to go. The shooter was out there, and there was smoke coming in by the back door. Was the killer trying to force them out the front door?

A few seconds later, he grimly dismissed that idea.

Smoke had started to pour in under the front door. The idea evidently wasn't to smoke them out. No. The killer had no interest in luring them out into the open.

The sadistic person waiting outside the house had decided to burn them to a crisp. And the fact that there were innocent bystanders inside with him and Jess didn't seem to bother him, or her, overmuch.

"Seth. Now what?"

Seth winced at Jess's hoarse voice.

He was out of ideas.

They were trapped.

THIRTEEN

Her lungs were burning. She blinked to clear her vision. It did no good. Water continued to pool in her eyes. A blurry shape was coming her way, wriggling like a large caterpillar. Seth. He army-crawled to her.

She blinked again as he put his face a couple of inches from hers.

"Are you okay?" he mouthed. How she wished she could hear his voice!

She nodded, but it was a lie. No, she wasn't okay. She was terrified. And in pain. But he didn't need to know that. Why place that burden on him when he couldn't change the circumstances? He yelled something at Levi.

Squinting, she was just able to see her old friend pointing. When Levi started crawling toward the other side of the house, Seth gestured for her to follow.

A spark of hope lit inside her soul. Could there be another way out? With renewed vigor, she crawled after Levi, praying as she struggled along. Every few feet, she glanced back over her shoulders, heartened to see Seth coming along behind her. He could have moved faster if he was ahead of her. But he wouldn't do that. The man she had come to know and trust in the past few days would never take the chance that she would be left behind.

Immediately upon entering the room, she noticed a decrease of smoke. Seth came in behind her and closed the door. That would buy them a few extra minutes.

Levi waved Seth forward, and together the two men pushed an oval area rug out of the way. A wooden trapdoor was revealed. It had a single slide latch lock near the bottom corner.

The cellar.

Jess hadn't seen it in so many years, she had entirely forgotten it existed.

The two men cleared the rug the rest of the way off the door and Levi wrestled with the latch. *Come on, come on,* she urged silently. The lock was stuck. It would open. It had to. She refused to believe they had come this far, only to die now. Frantically throwing her glance around the room, she spied a large tool near the wood basket. A maul. For splitting wood. A weird place to find such a tool. But she didn't have time to wonder about it now.

"Seth!"

His head whipped toward her and she pointed at the maul. His face cracked into a relieved grin. Grabbing the maul, he marched to where Levi was. Levi backed off to allow him to swing at the latch. It was lifted clear off the door with the first blow. Levi opened the door, wrinkling his nose.

A second later, so did Jess. The rank odor of mold and stale water rose out of the cellar and assaulted her nostrils. The rain had flooded the cellar.

Jess shuddered, a horrible realization slamming into her. The open door yawned before her, leading into a dark, swampy pit. She was going to have to wade through the dark again. Her life depended on it. Fear held her legs paralyzed.

The two men hadn't noticed her predicament yet. Instead, they were rounding up candles and matches. Levi lit his candle. The flame danced, flickering like it was laughing at her cowardice.

Seth lit a second candle. He turned to her, an expectant smile curling the corners of his mouth. The smile faded as he took in her frozen posture. Concern etched itself on his handsome features.

"Jess?" He signed as he spoke. No wonder. Smoke was starting to come in under the door. The air was beginning to get hazy. "Jess, we have to go, honey. This is our only chance."

"It's dark." She knew she was whispering, even though she couldn't hear her own voice. But she knew Seth heard it when his brows rose. Then his frown deepened.

"It's dark, yes. But we have candles. And we'll be together."

She nodded. Forcing her legs into motion, she gripped the hand he held out to her.

"Afraid of the dark?"

"And small places."

His eyes softened in tender understanding. The cellar was both. "Let's pray."

Astonishment flashed through her as he said a simple prayer. "Lord, protect us. Help Jess through her fear. Amen."

If he could surrender enough to pray, she could walk through the dark at his side.

They descended the stairs one at a time. Sandwiched

between the men, Jess alternated between feeling safe and wanting to scream as claustrophobia skittered down her nerves. She arrived at the last step and put her foot down into six inches of water. She was so sick of being wet. It sure beat being dead, though, so she held in her sigh of disgust.

The light from the candles danced, casting eerie shadows on the stone walls. She shuddered and tried to ignore them.

As he stepped down behind her, Seth placed his empty hand on her shoulder. She reached up and held on to his hand. The warmth of his palm sank into her skin, bringing comfort. She wasn't alone.

Sloshing through the ice-cold water, the weary trio made their way to the wall on the opposite side. If memory served, there should be a door leading to the outside there. If things went their way, it would be unlocked and easy to open.

Once at the wall, they followed the light slipping through the cracks in the door. Jess ignored the icy water which slapped against her legs and slipped over the top of her boots to soak her feet.

In less than a minute, they arrived at the door.

Apprehension settled in. What if the shooter saw them? Granted, the door was on the opposite side of the house. It was more likely that the shooter was watching the main entrances and the windows on the ground floor.

They were about to find out.

Seth joined Levi at the double doors and the two men shoved them open. Fresh air rushed inside, soothing her lungs.

Seth helped her exit the cellar. Jess was tempted to

tell him that she was fine, but allowed herself the comfort of his assistance rather than sticking to her pride.

As they emerged, a commotion near the front of the house drew their attention. Several Amish buggies were in the driveway, the horses placidly grazing on the grass while their drivers were working together to put out the blaze. Or what was left of it. A young woman wearing capris pants and a frilly top was talking a mile a minute on a neon-pink cell phone, waving her bangled arms as she talked.

Her mouth was moving too quickly to read everything she was saying. Her bright pink lipstick helped, though. Jess was able to make out enough to know the woman was talking to a 911 operator.

Reluctantly, Jess forced herself to survey the damage herself. She turned. And grimaced.

The front porch seemed to have taken the brunt of the damage. Black scorch marks clawed from the porch up the door. The doorknob had fallen clear off. She had no idea how the back door fared, but suspected it was heavily damaged, as well.

"Levi, I'm sorry—" she started, but he wasn't there.

Seth touched her arm. "You know he doesn't care about the house," he signed. "He cares that you are safe, and that his family wasn't home."

"But if I hadn't been here, none of this would have happened."

"Maybe."

The word pierced her. So she was to blame.

"Or maybe not. But aren't you the one always telling me God provides? He provided for us today, and no one was seriously injured. That's the important thing."

Jess opened her mouth, then snapped it shut when

she realized she didn't know what to say to that. God
had provided for them. More importantly, at least in
her mind, Seth was acknowledging His care. Blessings
came out of tragedy. She had read that several times in
the past. Now she was seeing it in action.

The amazement and wonder on Jess's face made him
squirm. And when she smiled at him, man, that dimple
just about did him in. He felt like a hero. Saving people had become commonplace given his job. He never
thought of himself as a hero before. But Jess was fo-
cusing those big hazel eyes on him and smiling softly
and now he felt he could do anything.

A siren rent the air. A fire truck swerved into the
driveway, and a crew of firefighters spilled out. A
couple of minutes later, an ambulance pulled up. Seth
closed his eyes. His chin sank to his chest as emotions
engulfed him. For a moment, he couldn't trust himself
to speak.

"Seth?"

Opening his eyes, he grinned at Jess. "Sorry. Just
momentarily overcome. That ambulance is from across
the creek. Which means the water has gone down. We
can go home."

He wasn't prepared for her reaction. Those hazel
eyes filled with tears and she flung her arms around
him, squeezing him tight. Smiling, he gently closed his
arms around her and hugged back.

"Anyone inside?"

The fireman's question, spoken to Levi who had approached the scene, broke the spell. Slowly, he backed
away from Jess. Reluctant to break the contact com-

pletely, he slid an arm around her waist. She leaned against him.

"No. We were inside, but we got out," Levi explained.

Seth nudged Jess, motioning with his head that they should move closer. Levi explained what had happened inside the house and how they had escaped. The neighbors gasped and exclaimed as they listened in.

A second siren shrieked in the distance.

"Police are coming," Seth signed to Jess.

She tightened her jaw and visibly stiffened her back. *She still expects to be blamed,* he realized. Without consciously deciding to do so, he caught her hand in his.

"Hey," he said softly, knowing they were close enough for her to read his lips in the waning daylight. "They can't accuse you of anything. You have an alibi and witnesses to everything. Do you understand me?"

She bit her lip and nodded. He relaxed.

"I know that. It's just that I haven't had the best track record with the police."

Leaning forward, he planted a soft kiss on the top of her head. "I'm here. I won't leave you to fend for yourself. Promise."

And he didn't. Even as the paramedics came and checked the three of them out, he stood beside her, insisting they look them both over at the same time. His arm was cleaned and bandaged. It was determined that the injury was fine, and wouldn't need stitches.

What was a problem was that both he and Jess had started to cough. Rough, harsh gasping coughs. It sometimes happened after being exposed to smoke. The police had finished collecting reports from the neighbors and Levi, since he was the only one of the three who wasn't coughing.

"We need to take you folks to the hospital."

Levi declined treatment, claiming he was fine.

Soon they were bundled into the ambulance and en route to the hospital.

Once there, they were separated while they were checked out.

Seth was relieved to see his brother-in-law, Dan, there, along with Gavin Jackson. Jackson was skeptical when Seth started telling about everything that had happened over the past two days. Dan, however, knew him well enough to know that Seth was not prone to exaggeration.

"Jackson, I want you to be in charge of making sure there is an officer looking out for Miss McGrath while she's here."

Jackson wasn't a fan of the idea. "Dan, do we really have the manpower for—"

"I'm not asking for your opinion. Do it!" Dan barked.

Jackson straightened his shoulders, he nodded, face blank. Pivoting on his heel, he strode away, speaking into the radio hooked onto his shoulder as he went. Seth watched him, uneasy.

"Will he cause trouble?" Seth queried. They already had their share of that and didn't need more.

Dan waved his hand, dismissing the idea. "Jackson's a good guy. A little hot headed sometimes, but he never stays mad. And he doesn't hold grudges. In fact, he's probably one of the most honest and hardworking men I know in the department."

"He doesn't seem to like Jess." He should let it go, but he couldn't. If Jackson's attitude put her in danger, he wanted to know.

"It's nothing to do with her. He has had some personal tragedies in the past two years. They have made him cynical. But he'll be fine."

Seth raised his eyebrows questioningly. Dan shook his head. "No, I'm not telling you. You may be my brother-in-law, but you know I don't tell tales."

He did know that. It was one of the things he liked about Maggie's husband.

A brisk footstep in the hall heralded the entrance of the doctor. He examined Seth quickly. Seth bore with it the best he could, tempering his impatience. He was fine, he knew it. All he wanted was to go and find Jess, make sure she was all right.

"Well, Travis, you seem to be fit, except for some irritation from the smoke. I think you should consider taking the next day or so off to let yourself recover, but then you should be fine." Dr. Adams typed something into his tablet before glancing up at his patient. Shoving his reading glasses up on his thin nose, he stared at Seth over the top of them. Patent disbelief was stamped all over his narrow face. "What, no objection?"

Although the tone was mocking, Seth didn't take offense. Any other time, he would have objected, or at the very least, let his displeasure be known. He hated taking time off. Too many people in this town thought he had it easy. As if growing up rich had made him soft. To compensate, he worked extra hard to prove himself. But now he had a more important goal than proving himself to those who didn't matter to him anyway.

"No, sir."

The doctor waited, but he didn't expand on his answer. Finally the doctor sighed. "Okay, Travis, you're free to go." The doctor made to leave.

"Wait, Doc!" he blurted.

"Yes?"

"My friend, Jessica McGrath, how is she?"

"Oh, she'll live, too. You can both go home. Remember, I don't want to see you until Wednesday."

He was good with that.

Hopping off the low bed, he made to go find Jess.

"Hey, Seth, you still haven't answered all my questions."

"Aw, Dan. Can't we answer them at Jess's house? You are going to give us a ride, aren't you?"

He swallowed a grin as Dan sighed hugely. "Yeah, sure. Let's go collect your friend. Than I can brief you and get home to my family before Maggie puts the twins to bed."

Dan radioed Jackson to bring Jess down to meet them in the lobby.

When she arrived, Seth couldn't resist the impulse to go to her. It was too strong. Ignoring the narrowed eyes of the sergeant standing next to her, he ran a tender hand down her cheek.

"You okay?"

"Peachy keen." He got an impudent wink for his trouble. "But I'm so ready to go home."

"I scored us a ride." Hitching a thumb over his shoulder, he indicated Dan.

"Hey! Is that all I am? A ride?" Dan's voice was insulted, but he knew better.

Jackson stepped up to him. With his back to Jess, he murmured softly to Seth. "Are you sure you know what you're getting yourself into, Travis? You might want to think twice about getting too friendly with her."

"Step back, Gavin. She's been through enough. And frankly, so have I."

"Whatever. It's your funeral." Jackson shrugged, but his mouth turned down.

So he wasn't happy with Seth's decision. That was just too bad.

Fortunately, they didn't have to ride in the car with him back to River Road Stables. Sitting next to Jess in the backseat, Seth heard her happy sigh as they pulled into the driveway. In the fading light, her eyes shimmered.

"Wait, Dan. Her front door is open. It wasn't open when we left."

"Are you sure it latched completely?" Dan asked. Putting the car in park, he slipped his hand into his jacket. Getting his gun.

"Yeah, I'm sure. I watched her turn the bolt. You know I wouldn't forget."

Dan nodded. Seth didn't brag about it, but he knew that his recall ability had frequently impressed those who knew him.

"You two stay here."

Dan didn't wait around for their response. He stepped out of the car and went to meet with Jackson. Together, the two men went to check out the situation.

Looping his arms around Jess, Seth felt her tremble. Lowering his head, he placed his cheek on her hair.

"When will this end?" she moaned into his shoulder.

He had no answer. All he could do was hold her.

FOURTEEN

An hour later, she was able to enter her house. Lieutenant Willis—Dan, as he'd told her to call him—met her at the door. The compassion in his gaze almost did her in. Without thought, she stepped back so she was touching Seth, her arm to his. Just the warmth of him through her shirt steadied her. Gulping in a deep breath, she let it out slowly.

"Miss McGrath, I'm afraid your home was invaded while you were gone. It's difficult to say when it happened. There's been some damage. I will need you to take inventory of anything that might be missing."

Some damage? She walked through her house like a zombie, paying the cops no mind as she surveyed her ransacked home. Icy fingers played up and down her spine. Her legs trembled. She had stopped even trying to control the tears of anger and pain that slipped down her face and dribbled onto her shirt.

Every nerve ending was frayed.

Seth kept near her side, silent. For that she was grateful. She didn't think she could handle conversation at the moment. One thing she was really beginning to treasure about having Seth as a friend…he seemed to have a second sense about her, telling him what she needed at any particular moment. Not in a weird way. Just that he always seemed sensitive to her thoughts and feelings. No other man in her life had ever understood her so well. Not her father. Not Cody. No one.

"I don't see anything missing," she concluded after an hour. Slowly, she rotated in the center of her home office. The room that had taken the worst damage. Seth, Jackson and Dan all stood near the wall, watching her. They stayed silent. "Of course, there's so much chaos in here, it's a bit difficult to say, you know?"

Something niggled at the back of her mind. "Look, can I go put a battery in my hearing aid? While I think?"

As soon as Dan nodded, she darted into her room. Momentarily, she choked at the sight of her open dresser drawers, feeling violated. It was difficult, but she managed to put that aside as she fumbled for her spare batteries. Pulling her good hearing aid from her pocket, she inserted a battery and pushed it into her ear, nudging the rubber mold into place. And was rewarded with the low hum of masculine voices in the next room. Smiling for the first time in hours, she picked up the empty battery package and moved to throw it into the trash can beside her dresser.

Her smile froze on her face as her gaze fell on the empty cat bed.

"My cats!" She dashed from the room, crashing into Seth. Her fist, still clutching the battery package, slammed into his hard stomach.

"Oof!" His face reddened as he doubled over slightly. Oh, no.

Manfully straightening up, Seth gave her what was probably meant to be a nonchalant grin. What he actually managed was a pained grimace. "You have cats? How many? Who was taking care of them?"

How she had missed that beautiful, deep voice of his!

"I have two cats. Parsley and Sage. They are house cats, and very independent. I have an automatic feeding system, so they had enough food and water, and their litter was changed right before we left. I didn't ask anyone to come and watch them."

"Did anyone have keys to your house?" Dan asked, his face serious.

"Not that I am aware of." Panic scratched at her throat. She tugged at her collar in agitation.

An arm wrapped around her shoulder, pulling her close to a muscular side. Seth. She bent her head into his shoulder.

"Is there any room we haven't checked yet?"

Jackson. For the first time since she had met him, he wasn't sporting a challenging attitude. Was he finally starting to believe her? Or maybe he was just more sympathetic to cats than to people.

"Um, I don't think so. I went through every… Oh!" A hand slapped her forehead. "The basement. I never even thought of the basement. That was Cody's office. I keep it locked."

All three men straightened to attention.

"His office," Jackson said. "We went through that pretty thoroughly a few months ago. Let's check it out and see if you notice anything missing."

The whole group moved down the stairs to the office. When they were two feet from the door, Seth put a hand on Jess's arm.

"I hear meowing."

Joy filled her. Then it faded. If the cats were in there

that meant someone else had been, too. There was no pet flap in the door—for the cats to have gotten in, someone had opened it for them.

Tension filled the air as the policemen waved them back. Jess found herself with her back against the cold cement walls, Seth blocking her. Her hero. He was determined to keep her from harm, willingly placing himself in harm's way, again and again.

Jackson held his gun at the ready while Willis flung the door wide.

And two short-haired tabby kittens pounced on his feet.

"Gah!"

Seth hooted in laughter. A giggle welled up, both from humor and from the rush of relief as the bubble of tension around them burst. She couldn't help it.

"But…but, I don't understand," she managed finally. A stray giggle threatened, but she squelched it firmly. "Wouldn't the person after me risk blowing his cover by going through my house like this?"

Sober now, Dan and Jackson both nodded. "The killer doesn't care now," Seth stated, glancing back and forth between the cops. "Am I right? Enough has happened that whoever it is figures there's no use hiding."

He had said something similar at the house. She had so hoped he was wrong. But one look at Dan's face said his brother-in-law was in complete agreement.

Her fear was affirmed when he nodded.

"Yes. I hate to be the one to tell you this, but right now, the person or persons after you seem to feel you are a risk that must be eliminated, no matter what. Maybe they thought there was incriminating evidence here in the house. Get rid of the evidence, get rid of you, and our chances of catching them shrink."

She swayed slightly. Her breath caught, as if hot irons had pierced her lungs.

Yanking his cell phone out of his pocket, Dan started dialing. "I'm getting someone to watch over you for the night. Until we catch this guy, Miss McGrath, you need to be with someone at all times."

She heard what he didn't say, even as her freedom was again taken away.

If she didn't have protection, she would be dead. Just like her brother.

Seth followed Dan outside. Jess was in the kitchen, making coffee and something to eat. More to keep herself busy than out of any real hunger, he thought. He could read the claustrophobia looming in her eyes.

He grimaced. Claustrophobia. He remembered the fear that had paralyzed her earlier. Funny, he didn't remember her being claustrophobic. In fact, he remembered a field trip to some caves in high school. She hadn't been exactly social, but if his memory served, and it always did, she hadn't been scared, either. Just the opposite. She'd been fascinated by the damp, dark caves.

Something had happened to change that.

I was stuck in that small, smelly place for five hours until my parents and the principal found me.

It was his fault. Her fearless curiosity had been killed by his own careless stupidity. He had failed her, even worse than he had realized.

No. I can't dwell on that now, he thought fiercely.

Lord, if I could undo the damage I did to that sweet woman I would. Just help me to keep her safe. Please.

Quickening his pace, he was striding next to his brother-in-law in two steps.

"I need to talk to you," he muttered, cutting his eyes toward Dan, while keeping his face forward.

"Okay."

"Not here," he hissed as Dan started to slow down. "I don't want Jess to read my lips."

Avid curiosity and doubt mingled on Dan's face. But he followed Seth behind the car, much to Seth's relief.

"This is far enough."

"All right, Seth. What's this about?"

Seth proceeded to tell Dan all his fears about the killer possibly being a woman. The alert look that came to Dan's face let him know the other man was taking him seriously. He sucked in a deep breath. Now to tell the rest. "We learned from the girl who cleans house for the Harveys that they are skilled shooters. What I didn't tell Jess is that so is my aunt. Their house was broken into years ago and she freaked. Bought a gun and learned how to shoot."

Dan nodded. "When Miles gets here, I will let him know all this. Why don't you hang out until then? I can give you a ride back to your place after that."

"No."

Not much surprised a reaction out of Dan, but apparently Seth had managed it this time. The cop's blond eyebrows rose high over his gray eyes.

"No? Wanna explain that, Seth?"

No, he didn't, as a matter of fact. But he knew he didn't have an option. He needed to be straight with the man if he had a hope of convincing him.

"I need to stay. Jess trusts me. She doesn't trust Miles." When his chest hurt, he realized he was holding his breath.

Dan smirked. "Yeah? Well, if I remember correctly, last time I left you to play hero, you ended up with your head bashed in."

He sobered as soon as he said it. Both men were silent, remembering the attacks that had focused on Maggie, putting her life in danger over and over again. On that particular day when Seth had volunteered to help, Tony Martello, one of LaMar Pond's finest, had died in the line of duty, leaving a widow and two young sons behind.

He sighed dramatically, trying to lighten the somber mood. "You ever gonna let me forget about it?"

"Nah. That's what brothers do. Anyway, there's no real reason for you to stay. She'll be fine." He raised his brows. Seth knew that look. Dan wasn't fooled, and was waiting for the real reason to come out.

So he used his trump card. "What if she needs someone to interpret for her? I should stay 'cause I know how to sign."

He smiled, sure he had made his point.

"That a fact? Well, so can Miles."

"Since when?"

Dan smirked.

"Since always. Almost his entire family on his father's side is deaf. Grandparents, uncle. You name it. He grew up signing."

Deflated, Seth stared at him.

"You need to rest up, Seth. Take time off." Dan shifted his weight, getting ready to walk away.

"I can't." Dan tilted his head, listening. "Dan, a man should be allowed to protect the woman he loves."

There was, he reflected some satisfaction in catching brother-in-law off guard. Which was probably an understatement, seeing how Dan's jaw had dropped open more than he had thought possible.

"Love? You love her? Does she know?"

Seth shook his head even while he was speaking.

"No, she doesn't know. And I don't plan on telling her."

Dan frowned. "Why on earth not?"

"Really? Dan, you know how badly I messed up with Melanie. And my dad is a complete womanizer. You know how your own wife suffered because of his selfishness. My family has a history of disastrous relationships. Why would I put someone I loved through that? I can't take the chance of hurting her."

"Seth, you have more than made up for any past errors. As for your dad, you can't be held accountable for that. You are not him." Dan held up a hand, forestalling any protests that Seth might make. "Listen, buddy, I know how it feels to think you're unworthy of a woman. I felt that way for years. I was wrong. And so are you."

Guilt swamped him. He knew that Dan had almost let Maggie get away. He suffered from PTSD, and had some terrible issues to work through. But he had manned up and gotten the job done. Seth didn't know of another man who could bring such joy to Maggie's life.

Dan's hand on his shoulder brought his head up.

"I know you don't go to church, but I will pray for you."

"Actually, I would appreciate that. I think I may have gotten the God thing wrong."

A grin creased Dan's face. "See? You're learning already. Seriously, though. You were kind of a cocky jerk when I met you," Seth rolled his eyes, but Dan continued, "but you're one of the best men I know. I know that you mean the world to Mags. And the twins adore you."

"Yeah, they're great kids." Just thinking of Siobhan and Rory warmed his heart.

"Don't give up on love, Seth. You are worthy."

Dan ambled away.

"I'm not leaving!" he called after him.

"Yeah, yeah," came the response.

He stood outside for a few minutes after Dan left, just thinking. Could he possibly consider a future with Jess?

He wandered inside, deep in thought.

Miles arrived and parked outside, ready to stand watch to keep Jess safe. He could hear Dan briefing him.

The floor creaked behind him. Jess. She was drying her hands on a dish towel, anxiety emanating from her.

"What's going on?"

He walked over to her, taking the towel from her so he could hold her hand. He watched her face. If he needed to switch to sign he would.

"The cop who is keeping watch is here. Dan is telling him what's happening."

"Oh." It was amazing how much disappointment one little monosyllable could contain. "So, what now? Are you leaving?"

He hesitated. But only for a moment. He knew he was committing himself over and beyond what he should do in order to keep his distance, but it was like he had told Dan. He couldn't walk away while the love of his life was in danger. It just wasn't in him. So he opened his mouth and made the commitment. "No, I'm not leaving. If it's okay with you, I'm going to camp out on your couch."

The relieved sigh that burst from her went a long way to ease his heart. "I'll get you some blankets."

Instead of walking away, though, she threw her arms around him.

"Thanks. I know he's a policeman and that he's here to protect me, but I just wouldn't feel comfortable with him."

"He signs," he threw out, just to be sure.

Jess stubbornly set her jaw. "Nope. Doesn't matter. I don't know him. I know you. And I trust you."

And there it was. That one little statement was the best gift he had ever received in his entire life.

FIFTEEN

The following morning, Seth woke up at seven, an hour past the time he usually did. Several things clicked immediately. His body was one mass of aches and pains. His back was hurting from being crunched up on a couch too short for his frame. His arm was throbbing where the bullet had grazed him. Even his neck twinged as he sat up.

The second thing to come to his attention was the absolute stillness in the house. It set his teeth on edge. Rising to his feet, he found that the cats were both curled up, watching him with suspicion.

"Is your mistress up yet?" he asked, then winced. Talking to the cats? What next?

Working his way toward the kitchen, he noticed that Jess's bedroom door was open.

Worry shot through him. Despite his aches, he pulled his boots on and marched to the front door. Miles was gone, too. But his car was still there.

Seth felt his breathing and heartbeat speed up. *Slow down, keep your cool.* Forcing himself to remain calm, he observed his surroundings, keeping his mind alert.

Movement. Down by the barn.

Without hesitation, he started down the winding driveway that led to the barn. Pulling the door open, he saw Officer Miles Olsen standing in the aisle. The young cop appeared at home in the barn. It was easy to picture him working on a farm, mucking out stalls. Maybe he had, before he became a cop.

"Where is she?"

Miles jerked his head toward the tack room. "In there."

"Thanks."

Moving past the young officer, he entered the tack room.

Jess glanced up with a smile, and the sun came out for him.

"Hey. You weren't there when I woke up." *Brilliant, Travis. Like she didn't already know that.*

"Uh-huh." She shrugged and flashed him that dimple that drove him crazy. "I didn't want to wake you. I know you've been run pretty ragged. And I knew you were there, if I needed you."

Something loosened inside him. Only once the feeling was gone did he realize that he had been jealous. Jealous that she had replaced him with Miles. Which was ridiculous.

"Whatcha up to?"

"I missed the horses. So I came down to check on them. And it's a good thing I did. Kim never showed up today." A frown carved into her brow. "I can't understand it. Kim always leaves a message if she can't come in. I have a text answering machine. But she didn't leave any messages. I hope she's okay."

A cell phone rang. In the aisle, he heard Miles answer it. Although he couldn't make out the words, he could hear the tension and excitement in the voice. He continued listening, and wasn't surprised when he heard footsteps running toward them. A second later, Miles burst into the room.

"I just got a call from the lieutenant," Miles stated. "A green car like you described was found this morning."

Jess gasped. Seth was in full agreement with the sentiment. He felt a little like gasping himself. Except it wouldn't be manly. Finding the car, though. That could be a huge break in the case. If it were the right car.

"Are the two of you up to coming to take a look, see if you can ID it?"

Neither of them needed their arms to be twisted. Within minutes, they were tucked into the backseat of Miles's cruiser. Seth sat beside Jess, aware of her hands clenched so tight in her lap, the knuckles were bone white. Her left leg bounced up and down in constant motion.

Reaching out, he pried her hands apart and intertwined their fingers. She gripped onto his hand like it was a lifeline.

Flashing lights in the distance warned them that they were approaching the scene. Seth and Jess both sat up as Miles slowed the cruiser, veering expertly onto the shoulder behind the small green car with dark tinted windows. Sergeant Jackson was waiting for them.

Beside him, Jess's breathing grew harsh, shallow. The hand in his grasp trembled. The need to comfort her in some way tugged at him. But he had nothing. Instead, he offered a prayer for her strength and endurance as she faced this new fear.

Sliding across the seat to the door Miles held open,

they emerged from the cruiser and shuffled toward the car. Jess shivered. He tucked her closer to his side.

"No driver?" he murmured to Miles.

"We haven't found one yet. But the car is registered to a Keith Barnes."

"Keith!" Jess's voice was strangled. "That's Kim's older brother. But there's no way he was driving that car. He's in the service. Deployed overseas. He won't be home for months."

Seth's mind made a connection he didn't want it to make. But it was the logical explanation. "Jess, you said Kim never showed up for work. Is it possible she was driving the car, and that she was behind some of this?"

Jess started backing away, shaking her head. She stumbled over a branch. He grabbed hold of her before she could fall. He was surprised she didn't fight his hold, but seemed to melt into it.

"I don't want to believe it. But, Seth, she knew that I was going to be at your uncle's house. When I went to my house to pack, I left her detailed instructions, including where she could reach me in case of an emergency. I never thought I'd be in danger. Not in a house full of people."

"Reasonable assumption."

Poor Jess. She looked shattered at the possible betrayal by one of her staff.

"It's just a hunch," Miles called to Jackson. "But let's check the trunk."

In horrified fascination, Seth and Jess watched as the trunk was opened. A large black sheet was draped over the contents. His pulse thudded in his chest as Miles reached his gloved hand out and gently pulled back the sheet.

Black hair covering a pale oval face. A gunshot wound in the temple.

It didn't take a paramedic to know the young woman was dead.

Kim Barnes had been found.

The shock went too deep for tears. One of her employees, dead. In the car that had been following her for weeks. It made no sense. Kim hadn't even been in Pennsylvania when Cody had died. Her whole family was seeing her brother off in Texas.

It made no sense. None at all.

But then again, some of it did fit. Kim might not have killed Cody, but she did have access to Jess's schedule. And to some of their client information. Suddenly, her employee appeared more like a snake that had been deliberately dropped into her life. Why?

She didn't know how much more she could take. Thankfully, she wasn't alone. She had God. Her faith was being tested fiercely, but she wasn't letting go. And she also had Seth with her, a tangible person to hold on to when she felt the need.

But he was more than that, her mind whispered. She blocked out the murmurs. Her emotions were in too much turmoil to deal with her growing affection for the dark haired man sitting at her side.

She had positively identified the car as the one that had been following her. And she had identified the body in the trunk as her employee. Former employee. Now she just wanted to go home. What was the hold up? What else could she do?

"Here is your coffee, Miss McGrath." Lieutenant Willis and Officer Olsen sat down across from her.

"What are we waiting for? When can I go home?"

"Ma'am, we need to wait for the certified interpreter to arrive. She's traveling from Erie, and should be here within the next ten minutes."

"Where's Seth?" Oh, she hated showing weakness, but she really wanted Seth with her. Part of her was tempted to tell them that she didn't need an interpreter, but that was foolish. Of course she needed the interpreter. Lip reading could only work so far. And she only had one working ear, so to speak. This was too important not to understand everything to her fullest capability.

For a tough man, Lieutenant Dan Willis had an amazingly gentle smile. "Don't worry about Seth. He's still here. But we can't have him in the room while we talk to you."

A chill settled in her chest. Her heart stuttered.

"Am I in trouble?"

"No, ma'am. But we are looking at reopening your brother's case. I need all the information you can provide."

She was ready to scream by the time the door opened and a tall woman with sleek blond hair entered. She introduced herself as the certified interpreter and the questioning began in earnest. At one point, she was surprised when Lieutenant Willis let on that they had found large deposits in Kim's checking account. She was apparently being paid to spy on Jess. Hopefully spying was all she did. It would feel so much worse to know that the girl she had worked with and trusted had had a hand in the evil happenings.

"We haven't figured out Victor Horn's part in all this yet," the lieutenant explained. "He was fairly new to the area. He does have a record. Assault. Petty theft. We'll keep looking."

"Right now, we are working on a list of all the women at the Taylors' party this weekend," Officer Olsen interjected. "There are a few who stand out."

She reared back. "All the women? Why? Bob Harvey was the one going through my room. I would have thought he and his wife would have been among the first people looked at."

"And we *are* looking at him. He, his wife and Willa Taylor are all suspects." He slanted a frown toward his younger colleague. A frown that Olsen either ignored or didn't see.

"Besides," Olsen piped in, "Seth was pretty sure that the person talking to Mr. Horn before he was shot was a woman."

Right. They had talked about that before.

"And then there's the fact that Mrs. Taylor and Mrs. Harvey are both reputed to be the best shots of the whole party."

She couldn't breathe. All the air had been sucked out of the room, leaving her gasping. Lights swirled before her eyes for an instant.

Seth's aunt knew how to shoot a gun. Was skilled, in fact.

And he had never told her.

So much for trusting her, for being honest with her.

Lost in her feelings of betrayal, she barely heard the next sentence. Dimly, as if through a tunnel, she heard Lieutenant Willis offer to drive her home.

Nodding, she grabbed her jacket and walked beside him, feeling like a sleepwalker. Seth's face lit up with relief when he spotted her. Was it only an hour ago she was wishing for him by her side? What a joke. His smile faded to a puzzled frown as she stepped past him without acknowledging his presence. If she had opened her mouth, all the vitriol rising up inside her like a flood would spew out. Ignoring the hurt that slipped behind his eyes, she allowed Officer Olsen to hold the cruiser door open for her and slipped inside. She ignored Seth when he climbed in the backseat. Willis would follow in a second cruiser.

The car ride back to her house was awkward. She didn't care. She had nothing to say to Seth. Nothing.

Of course she couldn't keep silent forever. When the cruiser pulled up to her house, Seth started to climb out. Like he was going to stay with her.

As if. She wasn't having that.

"You don't have to stay with me. I'm not a baby." Ice dripped from her voice. It wasn't surprising. Her heart felt like it had been replaced with a chunk of ice. That was fine. It was when the ice began to thaw that she'd be in trouble.

"It's still not safe for you to be alone," he protested.

A shrug. "Officer Olsen can drop you off before returning."

Silence.

"Jessie? Honey, why are you acting this way?"

That did it. She advanced on him, fury pulsing through her veins like fire.

"Honey? How dare you call me honey!" She could just spit, she was so mad. "When were you going to tell me about your aunt's penchant for shooting guns, Seth? According to Officer Olsen, she shoots better than most of the men we know. Even while we were in danger, you were keeping vital information from me. And I can guess I know why. Because even as I thought we were becoming closer, that we might have found something special, you were choosing your aunt over me. Your vicious aunt who might have tried to kill me. Just like you picked your friends over me all those years ago. Every time I start to think I can trust you, you remind me just how little I mean to you, compared to the other people in your life."

His face lost every drop of blood.

"Jess, baby, let me explain. That wasn't it. I wasn't choosing anyone over you!"

She held up an imperious hand.

"Whatever. I don't want to hear it. Because I can't fall in love with someone who can't be honest with me. Someone who won't put me first. I just can't do it."

Whirling, she ran up the steps and into the house, slamming the door.

The tears were spilling out of her eyes, blinding her, as she fumbled with the deadbolt.

She had lied to him when she told him she couldn't fall in love with him.

She already had.

SIXTEEN

Jess opened her eyes the next morning with a groan. Her lids felt like sandpaper over her sensitive irises. It had taken her hours to fall asleep. She had soaked her pillowcase with tears before sheer exhaustion had won out. And when she did finally fall asleep, her sleep was restless, tormented by unsettling, disjointed dreams.

Which was why, even though she was tired enough to sleep on, she dragged herself out of bed. No telling what kind of dreams would chase her if she went back to sleep.

Wonder if Seth's awake yet?

No, no, no!

She and Seth were done. She was not going to waste any more of her valuable time worrying about that man. His sad eyes had haunted her last night. No more. Needing to keep busy, she made a pot of strong black coffee and filled a travel mug with the bitter stuff, pouring in an ample amount of mocha creamer to soften the punch. Then she poured a second mug and carried it to a very sleepy Olsen. The man was almost pathetically grateful as he took a deep sip.

Chores. Time to do chores.

She hurried to feed and water the horses. As she did so, she had time to think. Maybe she should have given Seth a chance to explain? Her mind drifted back to the times he had thrown himself in harm's way for her. And the way he had of holding her hand when she was frightened. She remembered his strength as he had climbed down the rocks without a rope. And his gradual acceptance of prayer.

The more she thought about it, the more she felt ashamed of herself. For all her hurt over being judged and treated poorly, she had turned around and done the same to him.

Maybe she could call him up later, and beg his forgiveness. She squirmed just thinking about it. What if he refused to talk with her? It would serve her right, but the idea of having egg on her face didn't appeal to her. Neither did the idea of letting him go without a fight.

If she had her cell phone, she could call him.

A shadow fell across her, startling her. Someone had entered through the side door.

Whirling, she found a familiar face. One she hadn't expected to see.

"Deborah! How did you get here? I didn't hear you pull up."

"Hello, Jess. I rode my horse over through the back trails." The other woman nodded stiffly. "I wanted to apologize."

Puzzled, she tilted her head and surveyed the blond. "What are you apologizing for?"

Deborah raised a slim hand and pushed her hair behind her ear. "Oh, well, for starters, I wasn't very nice to you at the Taylor house. I knew you had had a rough time. Everyone did. But I was worried about how everyone would talk if we were too chummy. It's been hard, dealing with the scandal of my fiancé's suicide and all."

Tightening her lips to keep the sarcastic words at bay, Jess merely nodded.

"I need to talk with you, Jess. Can we go somewhere and talk? Please? It's a great day for a trail ride. That would give us some privacy."

For some reason, Jess was reluctant to go. But that was ridiculous. She had known Deborah for years. Surely, it couldn't hurt to spend half an hour with her. Maybe when all this was over. She wasn't stupid enough to go anywhere with her while there was real danger lurking.

A car horn honked.

"Hold on, Deborah. I'll be right back."

Wiping her dusty hands on her jeans, she strolled to the doorway. Officer Olsen had driven his cruiser down. His door was open, and he was standing behind it. When he saw her he waved. And began to sign to her across the distance. Wow, his ASL was flawless.

"Bob and Lisa Harvey have just been arrested. The information you provided was enough for a warrant, and their house was searched this morning. They found evidence implicating them. I can't say what. Only that it looks like you are out of danger."

"So soon? That's great!" Doubt lingered in her mind. Even though he said she was safe, it felt too sudden.

"I'm also supposed to tell you that they are being charged with your brother's murder."

Stunned, she stared at the officer. Realizing her mouth was hanging open, she closed it with a snap.

"Murder." The word dropped from her lips like a rock. She had known it, deep inside. But to hear that

Cody had been murdered, the feeling was indescribable. She felt joy knowing the black cloud hanging over the stables was being lifted...and yet the joy was tainted. Cody hadn't killed himself, but he had been taken from her, just the same. And if what she knew of the Harveys was true, it was to protect themselves. What a senseless waste of a good man's life.

"What about the money that was stolen from the foundation? Did they take it?"

Miles shook his head. "Sorry. We don't know where the money is yet. But we'll keep looking."

"So, I don't need you to protect me, huh?"

Officer Olsen sent her a boyish grin. "Nope. It's been a pleasure ma'am, but I need to grab a shower before I head to the station."

"I understand." She sighed. "Well, that frees me up."

"Excuse me?"

"Sorry," she apologized. "Deborah—my brother's fiancée—is inside. She wants to go for a trail ride. I hadn't thought it was safe, but I guess it is."

Feeling pinned in, she returned to Deborah and accepted her offer. The last thing she wanted to do was go for a trail ride. But she supposed she owed it to Deborah to hear out what she had to say, for Cody's sake if for no other reason. And anyway, riding her horse might lift her spirits. Maybe clear her head. If she stayed home, she'd probably dwell on Cody.

That, and the mess she'd made out of whatever was developing between Seth and herself. Correction. Had been developing. Why would he want anything to do with her now after the way she'd rejected him?

Saddling Misty, she pulled herself up on the horse and followed Deborah onto the familiar trails.

"Let's go this way," Deborah said, pointing to the trails on the right. "It's prettier. The lookout point is amazing this time of year."

Since she agreed, Jess nodded. Clicking her tongue, she asked her horse to take the path.

Something niggled at her. Something she couldn't place.

Then she knew.

"That's it!"

Deborah pulled up beside her. "That's what?"

"Officer Olsen just told me that they have arrested someone for the attacks against me and for my brother's murder."

"That's fantastic!"

"Yeah."

"You don't sound convinced," Deborah's smile seemed forced.

"I was at a conference the weekend he was murdered. So were the people the cops have arrested. So either they were working with someone else, or the evidence is wrong."

"Jessica, you should never try to play detective. It's dangerous."

For the first time that morning, she really looked at Deborah. She still had the pretty girl-next-door face Jess had always known, but it seemed harder than she remembered. A horrible suspicion bloomed in her mind. Deborah was acting a little off. And she hadn't seemed surprised to hear that Cody had been murdered even though everyone believed he'd committed suicide. When she, his sister, had only heard less than an hour ago.

Just what was Deborah's real purpose?

Deborah edged her horse closer to Jess's. Too close. Panicked, Misty backed up, tossing her head.

That's when Jess noticed two things. First, they were on a high ledge. Second, Deborah had pulled a gun from her boot. And pointed it at her.

"Get off your horse."

Silently, Jess did as she asked. Keeping vigilant, she waited for a chance to make a move.

"You are such a nuisance, Jess." Keeping the gun steady, Deborah slid off her own horse. "All you had to do was accept your brother's death was a suicide. Cry a few tears. Then move on. I never would have tried to hurt you if you had. But, no, you had to go and start asking questions."

"How did you know I—"

Deborah scoffed. "Of course I knew. I convinced that girl to apply for a job at your stables, keep tabs on you and your brother. She owed me money, so it was easy to do. But she let herself get caught. I heard y'all were looking for her car. And I knew she was thinking of coming clean to the police. I couldn't have that. Now she's no longer an issue. Which is more than I can say about you."

Seth pulled his truck into Jess's driveway. He and Dan had gone to retrieve it from his uncle's house that morning. Thankfully, it hadn't suffered extensive damage.

Willa had been painfully humble after being hauled in to the police station for questioning. When it became clear that the police had reason to believe that Cody had been framed, her arrogant facade had crumbled.

None of that was important. As soon as he had his

truck back, Seth had hightailed it back to River Run Stables to plead his case with Jess. Ironically, it had taken her trying to toss him out of her life for him to realize that he didn't want to walk away. She had been right about one thing…they had started something special. Something he planned on keeping.

Shutting off the truck, he threw open the door and jumped out. The crunch of the gravel beneath his feet seemed eerily loud. There didn't seem to be anyone about. Picking up the pace, he jogged to her front door and pushed the doorbell.

Waited ten seconds. Pushed it again. He could see the blinking lights through the window. Lights that went off whenever the doorbell rang. So he knew it was working.

Where was she? And where was Miles?

He had a bad feeling about this. Really bad.

A police cruiser hummed up the driveway and came to a halt beside his truck. Miles stepped out.

"Hey Seth!"

"Miles."

The officer raised his eyebrows, flushing slightly at Seth's cold voice.

"I thought you were going to be here watching over Jess. Why did you leave? Do you know where she is?"

Miles held up both hands as if to ward off blows. "Easy man. It's all good. The Harveys were arrested this morning. We have evidence that implicates them."

Relief nearly swamped him. His Jess was safe.

"So why are you here, then?"

Miles smiled. "Just a formality. I have some questions to ask her to tie up some loose ends. Nothing earth-shattering."

"She's not here." Seth frowned.

"I had hoped she'd be back by now. She went on a trail ride with her friend, Deborah."

She was friends with Deborah? That was strange. They hadn't seemed all that friendly at the house party. In fact, he couldn't remember them even talking to each other. It had seemed more like Deborah was avoiding Jess.

Both men whipped around as a car roared up the driveway, screeching to a halt. Rebecca was at the wheel, and a white-faced Levi was in the passenger seat. Seth remembered Jess saying Rebecca could drive, but didn't like to. So whatever she had to say, it must have been urgent. His pulse spiked.

Throwing the door open, she hopped out, leaving the car running. Levi reached over and turned off the ignition before jumping out to join them.

"Where's Jess?" She signed, without stopping to greet them.

"Out with Deborah," Seth signed back.

Rebecca's fine features paled. "No! She's in danger," she insisted.

Danger? Seth clenched his fists. The hair on his arms bristled.

"What danger?" Miles signed.

"Levi told me the Harveys had been arrested. But they were out of town when Cody died at a conference. I know it, because Jess was there, too. I remember her telling me how awkward it was because they were so hostile. Levi remembered Laura telling him about an angry girl who had come to see them around the same time. It was Deborah. She had a man with her. Laura didn't know who. And she mentioned she had taken care of what they had been too weak to do."

"That's when I remembered where I had seen Vic Horn," Levi broke in. "I saw him with Deborah once, in town. She didn't look pleased to see him. I think she was afraid of being seen together, but he wasn't worried. I knew who she was—that she was Cody's fiancée—and I heard her call him by name. I don't think they knew I was there."

Miles didn't hesitate. He ran back to his car and dove in. Seth was at his heels. The blond officer gave him a speaking glance when Seth slammed into the passenger seat, but he was smart enough not to argue.

Rebecca jumped into the backseat, scooching over to make room for her brother. Miles rammed the car into reverse and roared out of the drive.

"Where do the trails lead?" Seth yelled, knowing Levi would sign for his sister.

Seth drummed his fingers on his thigh while he waited for the response.

"She says the left path loops out a mile and then comes back. Mostly fields. The right path goes up and around, and it looks out on the lower paths. It can be dangerous.

"That's the one!"

Miles nodded, face grim. His voice was stern as he radioed in for backup.

It didn't take more than ten minutes to find the place where the path started and park the car. But it felt like forever.

"We'll have to walk from here," Miles stated.

Walk? Not a chance. Seth took off down the path at a dead run, knowing the others would follow. He had been a runner in high school, and still ran almost daily. It wasn't long before the others fell behind.

Part of him thought about waiting for Miles to catch up. He was the one with law enforcement training and experience. He had the authority to place Deborah under arrest. Waiting for him was probably the legal thing to do. It wasn't going to happen, though. Jess could die in the time it took the others to arrive.

Leaning forward, he broke into a sprint, ducking branches and leaves. A thorn tore into his arm. He didn't slow down. What was a thorn when Jess was in danger?

He didn't ease his pace until he arrived at the fence along the road leading to the lookout point. Down below, he could see two people standing near the ledge. Too close to the ledge. Two horses grazed nearby. When the blonde waved her hand, the sun glinted off the barrel of a gun. A gun aimed straight at the heart of the woman who held his heart in her hands.

Miles arrived. He heard other feet. Expecting to find the Amish brother and sister, he was more than relieved to see Dan and Jace and Jackson.

Deborah shrieked below. Seth's blood froze. Jess was backed up as far as she could go.

They were out of time. He leapt over the fence.

SEVENTEEN

"Deborah, I don't understand."

She had always thought Deborah was a pretty woman. But there was nothing pretty about the woman standing three feet away from her, her arms held straight out, the gun unwavering. Her lips were curled in a sneer. Tossing her head back, she shifted her stance, realigning the gun and staring down the barrel.

Hunter's eyes. How could she have missed the feral gleam? They glinted with unrelenting purpose.

She's going to kill me! If I don't do something, this will be the end of my life.

Seth. More than ever, now when it was too late, she regretted the way they had left things last night. She would never be able to tell him she loved him.

Stop it. Think, Jess. The situation was grim, but that didn't mean she had to give up.

"I've known you for years, Deb. You were going to marry my brother."

Deborah made a disgusted face. "Cody. What a pathetic excuse for a man he was. Always going on about God. And his obsession with those horses! He was a fool not to see the possibilities. All he cared about was that the horses weren't being treated properly. But what about me?"

The shriek she uttered was picked up and amplified by her hearing aid. The harsh sound reverberated inside her skull. Jess winced.

Maybe she could reason with Deborah. She doubted it, but at the moment, she was out of other options.

"Deborah, Cody loved you," she began, forcing her voice to remain level. "He—"

"Enough!" The other woman waved the gun. "What do you know? He broke up with me and was going to turn me in to the police."

What? Disbelieving, she shook her head.

Deborah nodded, smirking. "You never even guessed. He was always protecting you. But me?" She shook her head. "No. I tried to explain it to him. I promised I would return the money. As soon as my debts were paid, I would make good. But that wasn't enough for him. No, Cody McGrath was ashamed of me. How dare I gamble? How dare I steal from the foundation? Like he had never had problems. He was supposed to stand by me."

She stepped closer to Jess. Jess moved back, but found herself pressed up against the wall. In seconds, the gun was in front of her face. Swallowing, Jess tried to pray. Her mind was blank, her mouth dry. All she could do was repeat *Help me, Lord*, again and again.

"Did you kill Cody?"

It wasn't until the words blurted from her that she realized she was going to ask.

Ice crawled up her skin as the woman she had once thought would be her sister-in-law tipped her head back and laughed—a bitter, angry sound.

"I had no choice. He was going to go to the police. Expose me. What was I supposed to do? He would have ruined my life." She smiled, an unpleasant slash across her face. "I had Vic Horn help me. He would have done anything I asked. Plus, he enjoyed gambling himself. It wasn't hard for the two of us to stage the suicide. Unfortunately, Vic became cocky. When I lured you to the kitchen at the Taylor house, he was supposed to kill you and dispose of your body. Not drag you into a freezer. I would never have been so clumsy. But what can you expect from a man?" A dainty shrug and a sniff accompanied the words.

This was not the woman she'd thought she knew. Not a trace of the woman her brother had once loved was evident in the cold-blooded killer facing her.

The cold way she related the facts chilled Jess.

Deborah took a step nearer. Another foot and Jess could make a grab for the gun. She'd lose, no doubt, but if she was going to die, she'd do it fighting.

"And the Harveys?"

Deborah shrugged one slim shoulder. Careless. Almost casual. As if the lives of the ornery couple didn't matter at all.

"Oh, they're pathetic. So afraid of their own shadows. They were cheating the foundation, that much is true, but they'd never have the guts to kill anyone. The fact that your brother had turned them in for abusing their racehorses didn't hurt. And the fact that there was evidence that they had used steroids on their racehorses. They were easy scapegoats." Her painted mouth tightened. "But you had to stir the pot, didn't you? You could give them an alibi, so the police would have to keep looking. I had toyed with the idea of letting you live.

Even this morning, I thought if I could just get you to let it go. But I couldn't take the chance that you would conveniently remember something that would send suspicion my way. And I knew you were too much of a Goody Two-shoes to take money to look the other way."

Heat rose in her belly.

"You wanted me to take money to forget that you killed my brother? And Kim? Even your partner? Three people, dead, and I was supposed to be okay with that?"

"If you valued your life, you would have. But it's just as well. I couldn't have relaxed knowing you might decide to let your conscience win at any given moment. So I guess it's goodbye, little Jess. It's been fun."

The deadly calm with which Deborah shifted the gun made Jess's blood curdle. She knew that if the gun fired, it would be fatal. No more time. She tensed to dive for Deborah.

"No!"

Seth!

Deborah jerked back as the shout broke through the stillness. The gun wavered, moving off Jess for a moment.

Hope flared briefly in her soul. It died and panic took its place as Deborah whirled back, determined in her fury.

CRACK!

An agonized shriek was ripped from Deborah as the gun was shot out of her hand. Jess was vaguely aware of the cops swarming over the fence and running their way.

"No! I can't go to jail. I won't!"

Blood streamed from her hand and left a trail on the rocks and grass as Deborah charged the few feet toward

Jess. The force of her motion pushed Jess off balance. Wrapping her surprisingly strong arms around Jess, Deborah teetered on the edge of the cliff.

With a feeling of déjà vu, Jess remembered watching Vic Horn topple off a cliff into the river. Was she to suffer the same fate?

Seth was so close. With renewed vigor she fought. And for a second, she thought she was making progress. But then Deborah stuck her leg out and swept Jess's feet from beneath her. They both tumbled over the edge.

"Jess!"

Seth ran to the ledge. Terror grabbed hold of him. She was lying on the ground below. There was no movement. Was she dead?

Using every ounce of skill he possessed, he climbed over the edge and started a slow, painstaking descent. Rocks cut into his hands, reminding him that he wasn't wearing any protective gloves. Someone shouted after him. He tuned it out. He needed to get to his girl.

Shoving all fear, all his agony out of his mind, he focused on the task at hand. In his mind, a litany of prayer streamed out without his conscious decision. Every step down, every move, took him closer to his goal. It was probably the fastest descent of his life, but it felt like it took hours to reach her.

Finally, he reached the bottom. Dropping to the ground, he rushed over to Jess. She was just beginning to stir. Her eyes were flickering open. She was battered. Bruised. Looked like she had been through an earthquake. He thought she had never looked more beautiful.

"Jessie, are you okay? Honey, can you hear me?" he called urgently. At the same time, he was examining her for injuries. His hands shook wildly as he touched her. Never before had they trembled so while examining a patient. But then, he'd never been in love like this before. When he could ascertain no external injuries, he heaved a sigh but reminded himself that she wasn't out of danger yet. There could still be internal injuries.

"Seth." Just his name in her breathy voice. But it brought him to his knees. Her eyes focused on his face.

"Baby, I thought I had lost you." Blinking back tears, he grabbed a hand and kissed it.

"Seth. I was wrong. I didn't mean what I said."

"It's okay, baby. It's okay. Look, they are going to get you to the hospital. Check you out. But I'll be there. The whole time."

A smile flashed across her face. It was faint, followed by a grimace. "'Kay," she murmured. "Love you."

What? Had he heard her right? He couldn't ask, because she had fainted.

The next hour was filled with anxiety. Deborah had not survived the drop. Her head had hit the rocks when they fell. As awful as her actions were, Seth was sorry that she had died. He knew it would grieve Jess.

It took some maneuvering to get Jess out of her precarious position so that she could be loaded onto a stretcher. Every groan of pain that escaped her lips was a knife in Seth's heart. If he could have traded places for her, he would have. In an instant. All he could do was murmur encouragement to her. And pray. At the hospital, she was poked, prodded and x-rayed.

He was forced to wait in the hall while they examined her, as if they didn't all know him. He could feel a scowl etching itself on his face, but he didn't care. He had promised her he would stay with her.

Dan and Maggie had come to the hospital, too. Right now they were in the cafeteria getting coffee and something to eat. Maggie said he needed fortification. The best he could do was pace as he waited.

And waited.

An hour into the wait, he heard familiar footsteps in the hall. His dad. What was he doing here?

Senator Joe Travis walked to Seth and put a hand on his shoulder.

"You okay, son?" Seth was shocked at how softly his dad spoke. Joe Travis was always boisterous, confident. Now he seemed unsure of himself. "Maggie called me. Explained about your friend. I was worried."

His dad was worried for him. Would wonders never cease? He didn't blame Maggie for calling their dad. Her relationship with him was even more strained than Seth's, but family was important to her.

"I'm okay." His voice was little more than a husky whisper. Clearing the emotion from his throat, he tried again. "I appreciate you coming."

Sorrow filled his father's face. "I'm ashamed that you felt you couldn't ask me yourself. I know I've made mistakes, Seth. Bad ones. Mistakes that have hurt you. Hurt your mother, and so many others. But I'm still your father, and I care about you."

Seth's eyes widened in shock. His father never talked about emotions. Or admitted wrongdoing.

"I love Jess." Hadn't planned on saying that. But it felt right. "I want to ask her to marry me, but—"

Joe Travis sighed, and seemed to age before his eyes. "You're afraid you'll turn out like me, aren't you? Son, you are nothing like me. I'm both proud of you and ashamed of myself. You will never betray the woman you love."

"What about you, Dad?"

His dad didn't even pretend to misunderstand. "I know you won't believe this, son, but I have regretted my behavior deeply. I can't change what I've done, but I'm trying to be a better person. I have grandkids now. And hopefully, soon a daughter-in-law."

Seth smiled, feeling more at peace than he had in a long time.

"Wait with me? I promised Jess I'd be here for her."

Soon after, they let him go in and see her. She was asleep. He settled back in a chair and continued his vigil. He was there when she opened her eyes.

"Hi," he signed at her. Man, his poor Jess had taken a beating. As long as she was alive. She had a broken rib. And a number of cuts and bruises. The doctors were all amazed at how few injuries she had sustained from her plunge. He wasn't though. He was learning that God was bigger than their circumstances.

"Hey."

How exactly did he ask her if she meant what she said?

Then it hit him. He couldn't just sit back and expect her to say it again. He had to give, too. His throat constricted. Rejection was not a good feeling, and he still had the fear that his affections would be rejected. But he owed it to her to at least try.

"I'm so sorry for not telling you everything. You mean everything to me. I will always choose you over everyone from now on." He swallowed, holding her wide eyes captive with his own. Then he raised his hand in a single sign. His thumb, index finger and little finger extended while his middle finger and ring finger folded over across his palm. "I love you."

He braced himself for rejection. Or the infamous "let's be friends" speech.

Her eyes brightened with tears. But they didn't overflow. Her lips trembled as she smiled at him, showing that dimple that absolutely slayed him. Then, almost shyly, she raised her hand and returned the gesture. "I love you, too."

Leaning forward, he kissed her gently, taking his time. After all, they had all the time in the world now.

EPILOGUE

Seth held hands with Jess as they meandered through the small crowd of family and friends who had come to celebrate with them. Jess laughed at something his sister said to her, and he smiled in response to the joyful sound.

He couldn't remember half of what the guests had said. His mind was completely occupied by watching the lovely woman glowing at his side. His bride. Pride swelled in his chest. As of three hours ago, she was now his wife.

How on earth had he gotten so blessed?

He said a quick prayer of thanksgiving and marveled. So much had changed in the past six months. He was in love, had returned to church and was even making some progress in healing the breach between himself and his father. Not that the last one was easy. Joe Travis wasn't an easy man to have as a father. But knowing he had a Heavenly Father helped him to deal with the one he was given here on Earth.

"It was a beautiful wedding, Seth," a soft feminine voice said to his right.

He turned. He hadn't heard Willa and Ted approach.

"Thanks." He shook hands with his uncle, and allowed his aunt to kiss the air by his cheek. Then he smiled again when Ted grabbed Jess in a warm hug and smacked a fatherly kiss on her cheek. Willa smiled stiffly. She was trying, Seth admitted, but it might take a bit more time before the women felt easy in each other's presence.

"Thanks, Uncle Ted, for letting us have the reception here at your house."

"No problem. What else could I do for my favorite nephew?"

Yeah, yeah. Only nephew. But that didn't matter.

Satisfied, he glanced around. Maggie and Dan were there with their kids, Rory and Siobhan. No one looking at Dan with the kids would know that he was their adopted father. And the twins adored him. Maggie glowed as she stood next to her husband. Neither she nor Dan could stop smiling. Their smiles were contagious. Seth felt his own lips stretching into a grin. He knew why they were so happy. Maggie had confided to him that they were expecting a baby in seven months. The thought of being an uncle again filled him with joy.

As he watched, Siobhan left Dan's side and ran across the yard. Guests parted, smiling as the toddler rushed to where her grandfather was sitting with some out of town relatives and scampered up into his lap. Joe smiled at her, his eyes creasing as he gave her a hug. Then he slyly handed her a cookie from his plate. Had Maggie seen?

He switched to look at Maggie. Yep. She rolled her eyes, and laughed.

Unbelievably, Joe Travis was becoming a doting grandfather.

His gaze moved to the couple standing next to Dan and Maggie. Seth's former fiancée, Melanie, was there with her husband, Jace, and their infant daughter, Ellie. She was named after Jace's sister who had died tragically as a teenager. Even Irene, Jace's widowed sister, was there with her two boys.

"Chief Paul!" Matthew, the younger of her boys called, grinning, as he spotted LaMar Pond's chief of police, Paul Kennedy, coming their way. Both boys eagerly moved forward to hug their dad's longtime friend. Irene hung back, but she watched her boys, a sad smile on her lips.

Paul rustled the hair of AJ, her oldest son, and chucked Matthew under the chin before he moved past them to go stand with Dan. Soon, Jace wandered over and the three were deep in conversation. Football was probably the topic, judging by the intensity of the discussion. That and the commiserating eye rolls of their wives.

Rebecca sidled up to Jess, looking very pretty in her blue maid-of-honor dress. His eyes narrowed at the excitement and nervousness that filled his wife's face.

"Are they here?" she signed to Rebecca.

Flicking her eyes toward him, Rebecca nodded slightly.

"Who?" Seth asked.

"You'll see," Jess said in a sing-song voice. His eyes narrowed. His woman was planning something. His wife, he corrected, grinning. His wife.

He was sure of it when she motioned him to stay there and rushed out behind Rebecca. What was going on? Dan and Jace joined him, eyebrows raised. He shrugged to say he had no idea.

His surprise increased as Rebecca returned and nodded to Miles. The officer left the place where he had been talking to Jackson and moved to the side of the temporary stage. Directly in front of the table where Ernie and a group of Jess's deaf and hard-of-hearing friends sat. Rebecca sat down with them, her eyes on Miles. It was clear he had been asked to interpret something.

A minute later, Jess reappeared and hurried to the DJ's stage. After a brief whispered conversation, the man grinned and handed her the microphone with a small bow.

What?

"Ladies and gentlemen…may I please have your attention?" Jess's voice carried across the yard, and the guests slowly quieted, turning to watch the stage. "I have a special surprise for Seth. I am so grateful that God has blessed me with such a wonderful husband. And I know that there is one thing that Seth has wanted for several years now."

Puzzled, he tilted his eyes. What did he want? Besides her, of course. And now that he had her, his life was perfect. Except…his eyes widened, heart pounding. He had a sudden idea, a crazy idea, of who her surprise guest was.

"With the help of my father-in-law, I was able to hire a private detective. It has taken almost six months, but I am pleased to say he was successful. I would now like to introduce Seth to his little sister, Carrie Jones, and her guardian and half sister, Audrey."

His blood roared in his ears as Seth moved in a trance toward the stage. He barely even looked at the lovely woman with strawberry blond hair who entered the room. His attention was focused on the teenager beside her. Carrie. His half sister. Her blue eyes were wide and scared.

"She looks just like Sylvie," a tearful voice said at his side. Maggie. She had wanted to meet their half sister, too. Looking at Carrie, he agreed. She did resemble their murdered sister.

He reached the girl, and silently folded her in a hug. Maggie joined in, and the siblings stood for a few minutes just embracing. When they parted, he realized there were tears on all three of their faces. And on the faces of many of the guests as well.

There was a moment of awkwardness as Joe approached the group. Conversation stilled as he paused several feet away from his youngest child.

"Carrie," he started, then stopped to clear his throat. "Carrie, I know I have no right to expect you to be happy to meet me, but I'm your father."

The young girl stared at her wayward father. A minute ticked by. Then a slow smiled curled her lips. "I asked Mama about you many times, but she would never tell me much."

It was a start.

Jess arrived and planted herself at Seth's side. Sweeping her up in his embrace, he whirled her around, hearing her breathless laughter in his ear. He set her down, but took her sweet face in his hands and captured her lips with his. They were both breathless by the time he released her. The crowd around them applauded.

"I am so in love with you, Jessica Travis," he signed to her. "No one on earth knows me like you."

Jess, his sweet Jess, stretched up on her toes to kiss his lips softly. "I adore you, Seth. And I can't wait to show you each and every day just how much you mean to me."

Hugging her close to him, he shut his eyes, blocking out everything except the warm woman in his arms. Her scent teased his nostrils, soothing his soul.

He had come home.

* * * * *

If you loved this book, don't miss these other action-packed Dana R. Lynn stories:

PRESUMED GUILTY
INTERRUPTED LULLABY

Find more great reads at www.LoveInspired.com.

Dear Reader,

I hope you enjoyed Seth and Jess's story. While this is the third story set in LaMar Pond, it is the first book of a new miniseries which is connected by the local Amish community. I was glad to finally give Seth his own happy-ever-after. And a chance to play the hero. After seeing how much he adored his new sister and her kids, I had to find a special woman just for him. Enter Jess. Jess has been through so much in her life. She is by herself, but has confidence that she is not alone… God is always with her. Her faith has kept her going during all the trials thrown her way. It was such a joy to watch her grow closer to Seth, and in the process, help him regain the faith he had lost.

I was also glad to bring my experience of working with the Deaf and hard of hearing into the story. I had always toyed with the idea of having a Deaf character, and after having been challenged by someone close to me, I decided to take a risk. I have just barely scraped the surface of the richness of Deaf culture here, and I hope to be able to go deeper in the future.

Thank you for journeying with me. I love to hear from readers. Visit me online at www.danarlynn.com, or email me at WriterDanaLynn@gmail.com. I am also on Facebook, Twitter and Goodreads.

Blessings,
Dana R. Lynn

COMING NEXT MONTH FROM
Love Inspired® Suspense

Available May 9, 2017

SHERIFF
Classified K-9 Unit • by Laura Scott

Back in her hometown investigating the disappearance of a colleague, FBI K-9 agent Julianne Martinez doesn't expect to witness a jailbreak and become a target—or to work with her former love, Sheriff Brody Kenner, to bring in the fugitive.

AMISH REFUGE
Amish Protectors • by Debby Giusti

On the run after escaping her kidnappers, Miriam Miller takes refuge in an Amish community. Will hiding in the home of Abram Zook and his sister save her life—even as she loses her heart and begins to embrace the Amish faith?

CALCULATED VENDETTA
by Jodie Bailey

When Staff Sergeant Travis Heath rescues his ex-girlfriend, Staff Sergeant Casey Jordan, from a mugger, a killer begins hunting them. And with attempts on their lives escalating, they must figure out who has a vendetta against them...and why.

TEXAS TAKEDOWN
by Heather Woodhaven

Marine biologist Isabelle Barrows's research findings could put her institute on the map, but someone will resort to anything—even murder—to steal it before she can present it at a conference. And her only hope of surviving is relying on her former friend, Matt McGuire, for help.

CRASH LANDING
by Becky Avella

After stumbling on a drug-smuggling operation, rancher Sean Loomis and pilot Deanna Jackson must flee. But with men trying to kill them and a dangerous wildfire raging around them, can they make it out with their lives?

SHATTERED SECRETS
by Jane M. Choate

Narrowly escaping thugs who held her at knifepoint, lawyer Olivia Hammond turns to the man who once broke her heart, bodyguard Sal Santonni, for protection. But can they find her kidnapped boss and track down the person who's after Olivia before the attacks turn fatal?

LOOK FOR THESE AND OTHER LOVE INSPIRED BOOKS WHEREVER BOOKS ARE SOLD, INCLUDING MOST BOOKSTORES, SUPERMARKETS, DISCOUNT STORES AND DRUGSTORES.

LISCNM0417

Get 2 Free Books,
Plus 2 Free Gifts—
just for trying the _Reader Service!_

YES! Please send me 2 FREE Love Inspired® Suspense novels and my 2 FREE mystery gifts (gifts are worth about $10 retail). After receiving them, if I don't wish to receive any more books, I can return the shipping statement marked "cancel." If I don't cancel, I will receive 4 brand-new novels every month and be billed just $5.24 each for the regular-print edition or $5.74 each for the larger-print edition in the U.S., or $5.74 each for the regular-print edition or $6.24 each for the larger-print edition in Canada. That's a savings of at least 13% off the cover price. It's quite a bargain! Shipping and handling is just 50¢ per book in the U.S. and 75¢ per book in Canada.* I understand that accepting the 2 free books and gifts places me under no obligation to buy anything. I can always return a shipment and cancel at any time. Even if I never buy another book, the 2 free books and gifts are mine to keep forever.

Please check one: ☐ Love Inspired Suspense Regular-Print ☐ Love Inspired Suspense Larger-Print
(153/353 IDN GLQE) (107/307 IDN GLQF)

Name	(PLEASE PRINT)	
Address		Apt. #
City	State/Prov.	Zip/Postal Code

Signature (if under 18, a parent or guardian must sign)

Mail to the **Reader Service:**

IN U.S.A.: P.O. Box 1867, Buffalo, NY 14240-1867
IN CANADA: P.O. Box 611, Fort Erie, Ontario L2A 9Z9

Want to try two free books from another series?
Call 1-800-873-8635 or visit www.ReaderService.com.

* Terms and prices subject to change without notice. Prices do not include applicable taxes. Sales tax applicable in N.Y. Canadian residents will be charged applicable taxes. Offer not valid in Quebec. This offer is limited to one order per household. Books received may not be as shown. Not valid for current subscribers to Love Inspired Suspense books. All orders subject to credit approval. Credit or debit balances in a customer's account(s) may be offset by any other outstanding balance owed by or to the customer. Please allow 4 to 6 weeks for delivery. Offer available while quantities last.

Your Privacy—The Reader Service is committed to protecting your privacy. Our Privacy Policy is available online at www.ReaderService.com or upon request from the Reader Service.

We make a portion of our mailing list available to reputable third parties that offer products we believe may interest you. If you prefer that we not exchange your name with third parties, or if you wish to clarify or modify your communication preferences, please visit us at www.ReaderService.com/consumerchoice or write to us at Reader Service Preference Service, P.O. Box 9062, Buffalo, NY 14240-9062. Include your complete name and address.

LIS17R

SPECIAL EXCERPT FROM

Love Inspired
SUSPENSE

*The search for a missing colleague puts an FBI agent
right in the path of a prison break...and her
ex-boyfriend.*

*Read on for an excerpt from
SHERIFF,
the next book in the exciting new series
CLASSIFIED K-9 UNIT.*

The low rumble of a car engine caused FBI agent Julianne
Martinez to freeze in her tracks. She quickly gave her
K-9 partner, Thunder, the hand signal for "stay." The Big
Thicket region of east Texas was densely covered with
trees and brush. This particular area of the woods had
also been oddly silent.

Until now.

Moving silently, she angled toward the road, sucking
in a harsh breath when she caught a glimpse of a black-
and-white prison van.

The van abruptly stopped with enough force that it
rocked back and forth. Frowning, she edged closer to get
a better look.

There was a black SUV sitting diagonally across the
road, barricading the way.

Julianne rushed forward. As she pulled out her weapon,
she heard a bang and a crash followed by a man tumbling
out of the back of the prison van. The large bald guy
dressed in prison orange made a beeline toward the SUV.

Another man stood in the center of the road pointing a weapon at the van driver.

A prison break!

"Stop!" Julianne pulled her weapon and shot at the gunman. Her aim was true, and the gunman flinched, staggering backward, but didn't go down.

He had to be wearing body armor.

The gunman shot the driver through the windshield, then came running directly at Julianne.

She ducked behind a tree, then took a steadying breath. Julianne eased from one tree to the next as Thunder watched, waiting for her signal.

Crack!

She ducked, feeling the whiz of the bullet as it missed her by a fraction of an inch.

After a long moment, she was about to risk another glance when the gunman popped out from behind a tree.

"Stop right there," he shouted. "Put your hands in the air."

Angry that she hadn't anticipated the gunman's move, Julianne held his gaze.

"Put your hands in the air!" he repeated harshly.

"Fire that gun and I'll plant a bullet between your eyes," a familiar deep husky Texan drawl came from out of nowhere.

Brody Kenner?

Don't miss
SHERIFF by Laura Scott,
available wherever
Love Inspired® Suspense ebooks are sold.

www.LoveInspired.com

Copyright © 2017 by Harlequin Books S.A.

LISEXP0417